To Louise and Jeff

The Dragon King

Daniel Williams

Illustrated By Laurie Ragan

Copyright © 2012 Daniel Williams Laurie Ragan
All rights reserved.

ISBN: 1511491434

ISBN-13: 978-1511491433

DEDICATION
To Glenda, without whom this book would never have happened. Your spirit resonates throughout this work, guiding both the words and the paints that created it. We all love you and miss you very much. Rest in peace until we meet again.

Contents

The Dragon King

The Dragon King

Prologue

Eben stared at the framed painting of the dragon above his grandfather's huge stone fireplace in awe. He loved visiting the old house, so full of mysterious trinkets and treasures. There were flags and banners and shields lining the rough stone walls of the huge meeting hall. Swords and axes hung on racks around the room and there was even a set of armor that gleamed strangely, reflecting the light from the fireplace flames.

His friends all told him his grandfather was a little crazy, an eccentric collector of the long forgotten pieces of a world that had fallen into the shadows of time long ago. Eben knew better, though. He knew, as young boys sometimes do, that there was something very special about his grandfather.

That his grandfather had been trusted with a secret few people were allowed to know. He loved it when his grandfather told stories. He had never had anyone tell him stories the way his grandfather did. Everyone else read stories out of a book or, if they made them up they seemed fake and well, made up. Not his grandfather's stories, though! When he could get grandpa to tell him a story, and it wasn't often, many times he had to beg and plead and even offer to do chores around the huge old house to pry one out of him, but when he COULD it was magical.

His grandfather spoke as if he had actually been there, watching what was going on, seeing the action even as it happened. It was like Grandpa KNEW the characters he talked about, like he sat with them at the huge feast tables and ate and drank wine and touched the scales of the fearsome winged creatures he talked about. Eben would sit, spellbound, never moving as he sat in front of the fireplace on the old bearskin rug, hanging on every word of the story until Grandpa was finished with it.

Sometimes the stories weren't very long, an epic battle or a hero fighting for his people, but sometimes- and these were his favorite, the story would last all day. Sometimes they would even forget to have lunch, they were so wrapped up in the story. He had never heard the story of the Dragon, though. The Dragon that was staring down at him from the painting even now, his big yellow eyes holding his own spellbound as he gazed up into the fearsome face.

Whenever he had asked Grandpa about the story of the Dragon in the painting he always shook his head and smiled and said "Not today, Eben. That's a story for another time. How about I tell you the story of something else instead?"

Well, today was the day. It was the day before his eleventh birthday and when grandpa had asked what he wanted for his birthday he did not hesitate. He had looked Grandpa straight in the eye and told him he wanted to hear about the dragon from the painting.

The old man had stared back at him for a long moment, seeming like he was looking for something behind his eyes, his deep blue eyes looking searchingly into Eben's curious hazel ones. Finally he nodded and smiled. "Fair enough, Eben." He said in his soft, gravelly voice. "I will tell you the story. You're ready to hear it now, because you'll be a man tomorrow. Soon enough you won't have time for an old man and his tales any more, you'll be far more interested in the business of growing into a fine man yourself, which is the way things should be."

Noticing the look of fear in his grandson's eyes he chuckled and shook his head. "Don't worry, the stories won't be ending until you want them to. I have many more to share with you, but soon enough your life will become to busy and

3

you won't have time to listen to dusty old adventures, you'll be out making your own stories. I do want to share this one with you, though. I've been waiting a very long time to tell you this story, since it's a very special one. It's a story about a Prince who didn't want to be a King and a King who didn't have any subjects any longer. It's a story of love and hate, Heroes and villains, and sometimes people who were one while they were trying to be the other. It is not a story for a little boy and that is why I have never told it to you before."

Now, here he was, standing in the great hall, the fire snapping loudly on occasion as it warmed the huge, cold room, chasing away the chill of late November. The flickering oil lamps played tricks with the light, making the eyes of the dragon in the portrait seem to glow, even as they looked down at him staring up at them. He was so entranced by the painting that he never even heard the old man enter the room.

He jumped and squeaked in fright as he felt the gnarled old hand touch his shoulder lightly. "That is a painting of Araseth." Grandpa said softly, the reverence in his voice obvious. "He was the Dragon King. He was one of the finest creatures who ever lived. Why don't you sit down and I'll tell you about him?" With that the old man turned and moved stiffly over to his soft, comfortable story telling chair and sat down with a sigh, sipping a hot cup of tea and looking a the bear skin rug meaningfully.

Eben scrambled over to his place without a word, plopping down onto the coarse, dusty fur of the rug and wiggling a bit to get comfortable.

He smiled as he noticed the cup of hot cocoa sitting on a plate on the floor, waiting for him. He picked it up and took a sip, Grandpa waiting patiently until he had done so and settled in comfortably. The old man cleared his throat and began speaking, the little eleven year old boy caught instantly in the web of the story.

Chapter 1

In a world not far from ours lived a people much like us. They lived, they loved, they hated, just like we do. In this world there lived a Prince. At nineteen years of age he was much like any other Prince, in our world or in theirs, except for the fact he didn't really want to BE a Prince. Oh, he LOOKED like a prince, having inherited his finely chiseled features and sandy brown hair from his father and his deep, piercing blue eyes from his mother. He even carried himself as a Prince, even though sometimes he tried hard not to. Though he was not much larger than an average man, he seemed to be somehow bigger than them, an indefinable quality which always seemed to cause him to draw the attention he shied away from.

Point in fact, though, he was not happy with his lot in life. The life of an idle ruler did not sit well with Regan, this shown clearly by the fact he was deeply tanned from every possible moment spent outdoors, his hands rough and calloused from using a flint and steel and his arms corded with muscle from drawing a bow.

He possessed the same drive and spirit that drove his Great Grandfather, Conall, to do the legendary things he did. Conall, who had been the Hero who inherited the Realm, the one who had won the Throne, because he purified the Land of the Dragons who were wreaking havoc on the people and had then built an empire that none rivaled in all the world.

Prince Regan was of much the same character, his spirit larger than the King's courtroom. As is the way with many heroes of this type who find they are without a cause to fight for, however, Regan was bored and felt trapped by the entitlements of Royalty in peace-time. Where many lesser men would gladly have moved smoothly into the trappings of leadership, embracing their birthright and enjoying the fruits of their ancestor's labor, Prince Regan saw only petty people doing petty things, living petty lives with their only goal being to try to become richer.

Although he was expected to be a great leader who would earn the pride of his Ancestors, none of this really mattered to him. This Prince would rather be hunting. The woods were his true home and he always loved the chance to get out into them, away from the stuffy walls of the castle. He loved to breathe the clean air and mix with the people who had never been to a banquet or a ball and so did not know him by sight. He loved the challenge of living, not being served his life on a silver platter by a pretty girl who blushed and averted her eyes if he smiled at her.

He spent hours sometimes sitting in a different inn or tavern, listening to the voices of the common people talking about the lives they lived. In this way he had learned much of what their lives were like and the things they struggled with daily. Many times he had longed to speak up, to tell them he would speak to his father, that he would make things better for them, but he dared not. As soon as he spoke out all would know whom he was and he would not be able to go there again because it would not be the same. So, he sat quietly off in a corner by himself and listened and enjoyed and envied them their simple lives.

Not so today, however. Today the Prince had been summoned to sit in Court with his father. His father's health was failing and Regan knew it wouldn't be long before he had to give up his habits of slipping out of the castle to go live among the people where he was the happiest.

Chapter 2

Prince Regan sighed and fidgeted as he sat next to his father in the stifling throne room. His eyes wandered randomly over the masses of people assembled to address the King. He had urged his father to cancel court that day, since he wasn't looking well.

King Domnhal, once a large, strong man who had possessed the same sandy brown hair and strong features of his son, had been slowly failing over the past several months. The illness he suffered had shrunken his frame, laying waste to the former cords of muscle over his bones until it appeared that a mere skeleton covered in flesh remained. His once thick, sandy brown hair was thin and grey now, some wisps of it fading to a dull, lifeless white color as the life force slowly left his body.

Although he was clearly ailing, his stormy grey eyes remained sharp and focused and he was always present during the Royal court sessions, insisting the people of the kingdom came before his health always.

Prince Regan looked over at his father in concern when the King began coughing uncontrollably. A loud, rattling cough stole his breath from his body until he sat gasping desperately for air. The Prince looked over at one of the attendants and snapped at her. "Water for the King.. NOW!" His tone was harsher than he intended, but it had the desired effect. She quickly ran off and returned with a decanter and glass of water, meekly offering it to the King.

He sipped it, his cough tapering off finally. He took a deep breath, the air finally returning to his lungs and smiled at the girl then thanked her. When she finally walked away to resume her duties he looked over at Regan with an expression of disapproval. He leaned over and spoke quietly into his son's ear. "Regan, you could have merely asked the girl, instead of ordering her like you did. People will do what you order them to out of fear, but they will do a better job if you treat them with respect. You must always remember, son, they are our subjects, not our property."

Prince Regan nodded, properly chastised. "I know, Father. I acted inappropriately. I was merely worried for you." His father smiled at his son, still a bit weak from the coughing fit. "No need to worry, Regan. I'll be around for a while yet. I'll try to keep you from having to inherit the throne too soon. I fear the weight of the crown would be a burden on your head that would be difficult for you to stand yet."

Regan reached over and took his father's frail hand, nodding. "It would indeed, Father. I sit next to you when I am summoned to sit by your side and I still cannot understand how you can tolerate dealing with these ridiculous problems and quarrels every day."

He looked out over the seated crowds, the immaculately dressed dandies sweating heavily under their heavy garments in the front, the quality of the clothing lowering the further back the seated men went until finally, sitting at the very back of the room, the roughly dressed peasants and farmers sat patiently, waiting their turn to address the King. Most of those would never have a chance, though, the minor worries and concerns of the dandies in the front taking up far to much time for the poor men to ever have a chance to speak.

He leaned over and whispered into his father's ear. "Why don't we ever change the order around, Father? Talk to the men in the back of the room first. I suspect they have far more pressing concerns than the fact you have raised the tax on brandy or the newest garment order has been delayed a week. Those men should be out in the fields, yet they sit

here for days waiting for the slightest possibility you will
have a chance to speak to them."

His father looked out over the crowd, thoughtfully,
pondering the thought. "Perhaps we will discuss it later,
Regan. You make a valid point, Son. For now, though, we still
need to listen to the concerns of the people who are in line
today."   Regan sighed and nodded, acknowledging his
father's decision to speak of it later and the discussion
between the two ended as assembly business began
progressing normally once more.

Chapter 3

Later that same evening Regan held his father's arm as he helped him walk into the lavishly decorated banquet room, waving away the servants that rushed to assist. It was the night of the Feast of the Summer, one of the largest social events of the season. There would be members from all the royal houses attending.

Regan frowned as they waited at the doorway to be announced, looking over the sea of swirling colors of the fine, fancy dresses and the smiling faces of those who were lucky enough to be invited to attend.

His father looked over at him and smiled. "Why so glum tonight. Regan? You're young and quite highly sought as a prize among the ladies of the court. You should be having the time of your life right now. Go, enjoy! Have fun being the most desired young Prince in the entire world."

Regan nodded and sighed, shrugging. "I know, Father. The girls all fall over each other trying to gain my attentions. The truth is they bore me nearly mindless. I think every one of them has a head filled with nothing but air." His father nodded and patted his arm reassuringly. "I know. I got lucky with your mother. She wasn't quite.. um, typical royalty. I think there was a bit of dragon blood in her past somewhere." He chuckled, remembering the Queen fondly.

At that moment the Master of the Ceremony announced them. The King looked at Regan and smiled. "Well, try to enjoy yourself a little bit, even if having all those pretty girls falling over themselves for you gets a bit burdensome."

Regan forced a grin and nodded, helping his father into the room. "I will, Father, Worry not, I will try my best to not disappoint you." As they moved into the room Regan looked around slowly, meeting everyone's stares coolly, as if challenging them to comment on his father's weakness. Every eye was upon them as they ascended the stairs to the head table, which was heavily laden with all types of food and wine, as the orchestra played the royal processional music.

The evening had been every bit as horrible as Regan expected it to be. He was barely able to find time to eat or get a sip of wine as a seemingly endless parade of eligible girls had been brought before him, and he had smiled politely and nodded and danced with them as he was expected to. By the end of the night he winced noticeably every time he heard a giggle even though he forced a smile whenever he tried to engage one of the girls in conversation to make his father happy. Each one of them said exactly the same thing to him any time he asked their opinion of the slightest thing.

He sat heavily in the chair to the right of his father and poured himself a glass of wine, getting a look of shock and fear from the wine steward who rushed over to apologize for not being fast enough to wait on him. The king smiled at the man and waved him away, reassuring him his son was just impetuous and he hadn't been the least bit lax in his duties.

He leaned over and spoke to Prince Regan softly. "You must allow the servants to do their job, Son. Not letting him pour your wine for you made him look like a lazy fool in front of all the other staff." Regan sighed and nodded. "I'm sorry, Father. How you manage to remember all these things never ceases to amaze me."

He looked around at the rest of the people seated at the large table; many of them watching him with thinly veiled contempt. He sipped his wine and leaned back in the chair. "By the crown I will be SO glad when this night is over. I fear if I ask one more girl what she thinks of something and she answers me with 'whatever you think, Prince.' I will go completely out of my head."

The King chuckled and nodded. "I can sense your burden, Son. I've been thinking, why don't you go on a hunting trip? I know you've always been far more comfortable out in the wilds and I can see the burden of leadership is becoming a bit much for you."

Regan nodded gratefully. "If you think you'll be all right, Father. I could definitely use a bit of time to myself." Domnhal chuckled and nodded. "Oh, I think I can manage for a while yet, Regan. You go. Find yourself. To be a good King you first need to become a good man. Figure out who you are and the rest will come easily enough."

Chapter 4

The heat of the day was stifling as he moved quietly down the barely visible game trail weaving randomly through the dense, thick forest. The sounds of birds calling a warning at his approach and the many small animals quickly scurrying out of the path of his footsteps were the only sounds. Prince Regan's hair was plastered to his head and he had to frequently wipe the river of stinging sweat from his eyes from the effort of moving in the nearly impenetrable forest.

He paused for a moment to listen, cursing silently as a relentless insect buzzed in his ear. He smiled, thinking to himself, "No fit day for man nor beast out here, but I would still rather be in these woods no matter what the weather than be stuck in the audience chamber with Father." He shivered in revulsion at the thought of all those fake people, prancing and preening for their King, the reek of sweat and politics permeating the air. "When I am King court will be dismissed on days like this. No one should be forced to sit in a room and sweat like a caged animal."

His smile turned to a frown at the thought. Regan knew his Father's health was failing and he would be the one sitting on the throne much to soon. He shook his head, freeing his mind of the depressing thoughts. "But not today. Today it is just the woods and I." He inhaled deeply, enjoying the scent of the lush forest around him, the perfume of the wild flowers playing lightly over the heavier, musky scent of the decaying leaves and ferns. A squirrel rustled, high up in the trees, chattering a warning to its brothers that the human was back again. A bee buzzed lazily past his head on its quest for fresh flowers. He took a sip of flat, tepid warm water from the gourd at his side and made a face. "Hmm.. perhaps it is time to go get some fresh water. This has gone a bit stale."

He grinned once again, thinking of the always cool, clear, spring fed lake he knew of, only a couple of miles away. "Perhaps a swim, maybe some fresh fish for lunch. Yes, Definitely a good plan!" He moved then, not stalking this time, merely walking through the forest, enjoying the sights and sounds around him, his eyes scanning constantly, bow at the ready, always listening for any unusual sounds since it wouldn't do at all to accidentally trip over a mother bear and her cub or a wolf on the prowl for it's lunch.

Suddenly his eyes fell on an oddly crushed mass of ferns off to the side of the trail. He moved over to it curiously, examining the crushed and broken plants. His eyes widened in surprise as he knelt, his fingers tracing the outline of a huge track in the forest. He whistled softly in surprise as he slipped his hand into a single claw mark to test the depth of it. "Dragon? Inconceivable! There hasn't been a dragon about for centuries!" He knew that it could be nothing else, though. The stories had been passed through the generations. This was unquestionably the track of one of the great beasts all had thought wiped from the world long ago.

"I must tell Father!" He stood, turning to run back to the castle to sound the alarm. He paused. "But wait. For a print to be this size this creature must have been around here for years. It hasn't done us any harm yet. Perhaps I can just track it, get a look at it before I run back like a scared child and sound the alarm for just seeing a single track." His heart pounded in his chest as he thought about it. If he could find and kill one of those monsters by himself.. His family would be hailed once again as great leaders.

He knew there was some hesitation among the court as to whether he would sit the throne well. Some members of the Court thought he was not serious enough, not mature enough to take over for his father when he passed. Killing a dragon singlehandedly would remove all of those doubts and fears. He grinned widely, making up his mind, a wild, reckless mood taking control of him. He turned away from the path to the castle and lifted his bow, stalking carefully once more as his eyes scanned the ground for the next track in the forest.

He cursed softly. If anything the day had grown more stifling as he slowly followed the massive tracks through the forest. They had finally disappeared into a rocky stretch of the mountains. He searched in vain for nearly 2 hours before finally giving up in frustration. Now the shadows grew deeper as night began falling and he was miles away from home.

He sighed resolutely and made his way to the shore of the cool mountain lake. He fished for a bit, quickly landing 2 fat mountain trout for dinner. He built his fire and set out his bedding for the evening, merely some quickly cut evergreen boughs tonight, no silk sheets or soft mattress. After he ate he laid down for the night, listening to the sounds of the night birds calling over the water and the soft crackle and pop of his campfire. He drifted off to sleep quickly, dreaming about the huge beast that even now, watched him curiously from the other side of the lake.

Chapter 5

As the first rays of dawn painted the sky in vivid red Prince Regan sat up, blearily rubbing his eyes. He had not slept well the night before. Typically sleeping out in the night didn't bother him, he was under none of the same illusions as many of the town folk the night air was poisonous. Last night had been different, though. He could not shake the feeling something was out there, watching him sleep.

He stood stiffly, stretching as he moved to the edge of the lake and knelt down to splash water over his face to help him wake up. As he wiped the water from his eyes he looked out through the thick mist on the lake. Suddenly a dark, shadowy form slipped past, a vague outline in the mist of a long, serpentine neck with flowing sharp fins along its length, topped by a large reptilian head. He couldn't hold back a loud gasp of surprise and the head turned toward him for the merest instant, then, with a quiet splash it slipped out of sight under the waves.

He backed slowly to his pack and reached down blindly, feeling for his bow and an arrow, never taking his eyes off the rolling mist of the lake. He sat there for a long time, eyes scanning the mist as the sun slowly burned the fog from the surface of the lake. Finally, satisfied the creature had gone, he packed his meager gear and stood thoughtfully for a moment. His eyes scanned the mountains carefully. "Hmm.. The tracks from yesterday faded over there.. I saw the beast swimming in these waters today.. Its certainly rocky enough for there to be a cave around here somewhere large enough for the monster to live in."

He reached down and slung his pack across his back, nocking an arrow with a razor sharp hunting tip. "Well then, Sir Dragon, Let us see how well you fare against one of these arrows. They've never brought down game quite so large as you, but I wager a well placed shot will do the job." He left his meager camp behind, following the shoreline of the lake. As he moved he watched the mountains carefully for any sign of a cave. Finally, hours later, nearly at mid day he found something. A faint trail led up to what appeared at first to be a rock wall, but when viewed from exactly the right angle was, in fact, a crevasse in the side of the mountain. He approached it slowly, his soft leather boots making no sound on the hard packed dirt of the path. Regan paused for a moment, calming himself. Finally, he inched around the edge of the opening slowly, hardly daring to breathe. The cleft in the rocks opened into a narrow path, barely wider than the length of his bow. He muttered in disgust, seeing how small the trail was. "There is no possible way something as large as a dragon could fit down here." He sighed and started to turn away when he saw it. A single deep claw mark cut into a softer bit of dirt. Somehow the monster COULD fit down this path!

His heart started pumping harder and beads of sweat formed on his brow as he began moving down the trail. Perhaps he might get lucky and catch the monster snoozing on the sun warmed rocks like any lizard would! He continued down the trail between the rocks, not making a sound as he approached what appeared to be an opening. Suddenly the walls of the passage opened in front of him, revealing a small hidden oasis of life.

Huge rocks had tumbled down into the natural stadium from above and now stood on the valley floor, jumbled against each other. The floor of the natural glen looked like the wide-open mouth of a giant with bad teeth. Regan shook his head slightly, chasing the fanciful visions from his mind as he pressed his back against the wall, moving into the hidden oasis. Suddenly he saw it! The huge form of the dragon lay curled on top of one of the large rocks, his scales blending in perfectly so he looked exactly like any of the other lichen covered monoliths.

He appeared to be sleeping as the Prince had hoped, his great eyes closed, his sides moving slowly as he slept. Prince Regan went to one knee, drawing his bow back slowly so it wouldn't make a sound. He sighted carefully on where the great beast's heart would be. He held there for a moment, his fingers slowly relaxing to let the arrow fly straight and true. He was so focused on his target he didn't see one great green eye open lazily and fix him with its gaze. "I wouldn't do that if I were you." The deep, rumbling voice echoed through the valley.

Shocked from his concentration the Prince jerked, letting the arrow fly. The shot went high, arcing above the behemoth's back and clattering against the stones on the other side of him. He quickly reached for another arrow as the massive head of the dragon turned and stared at him. He nocked the arrow, quickly drawing the bow once again, pointing it at the dragon's head. He glanced quickly around the clearing. "Who said that?" He called out, admirably managing to keep any sign of a tremor from his voice. The dragon's eyes narrowed a bit. "Why, I did, of course. Do you see anyone else here but the two of us?" Prince Regan blinked in surprise. "By the Gods.." He muttered in shock. "You can speak?" The dragon sighed, a loud, rumbling noise and he nodded slightly. "Of course I can speak, Regan. Did they not tell you while they were telling all of the 'heroic' tales about slaughtering my brothers?

Did they forget to mention my mate begged for mercy and asked your great grandfather to spare our children even as he slaughtered my family? Did your Royal family not mention to you about how I cried for my family even as your

Great Grandfather was trying to kill me as well? Even as he gave me THIS?"

The great beasts wings unfurled in a heartbeat, a large, ugly swatch of missing scales and scar tissue appearing on his side. The arrow dipped slightly as Prince Regan took in the sight of the scar. He shook his head slightly. "They.. they never mentioned. All I was ever told was dragons are ferocious beasts that slaughter cattle and level villages." His eyes narrowed slightly, the arrow rising once more as he remembered the stories from his youth. The screams of the villagers, the panic, peasants screaming for help until his Great grandfather rode out to defend the Lands.. The Dragon stared at him for a moment and finally he nodded slightly.

"All those stories you heard were true, I'm afraid. There was some of our kind which did everything you heard about. Only two of them, but enough to doom our race." He chuckled sadly. "The thing the humans didn't know was those two renegade dragons were caught and executed by the rest of us for their crimes against humans even before the first human hunting party set out. It was far to late, though. The damage had been done. Your kind saw all of us as monsters after that. Your great grandfather hunted us relentlessly, leading his dragon killers into our dens and slaughtering us, one by one, until there are very few of us left in the world. " He stared at the Prince for a moment, resignedly.

"And now you, Prince Regan, Great grandson of the great dragon hunter, have come to finish us off once and for all. Where are your hunters, Boy? I didn't see anyone with you this morning." Prince Regan looked around, suddenly feeling very alone. "There ARE no other hunters, Dragon. I came to face you alone." He thought maybe, lacking numbers, sheer bravado would keep him from being killed for a while yet.

The dragon raised one eyebrow critically, studying the young Prince. "No others, hmm? And you came armed with THAT?" He eyed the hunting bow disdainfully. "At least Conall had the good sense to wear armor when he slaughtered us." Suddenly the dragon's head shot forward, stopping inches away from the drawn bow, examining the knocked arrow. "A STEEL arrow head? Oh, how the stories get muddled through the ages. Steel can't hurt a dragon, Boy. Didn't you hear about the great Onyx arrowheads the slayer used on us? Prince Regan suddenly remembered one of the songs from his childhood. "Ding Dong, the dragon died with the gleaming onyx deep in his side."

He sighed and lowered the bow, letting the string go slack. "As I matter of fact, now that you've reminded me, I DO remember something to a similar effect." He took the arrow from the bow, placing it back into the quiver. He slung his bow carefully on his back and straightened his shoulders, facing the dragon. "I suspect now you will be the one killing me, Dragon? I suppose its no more than I deserve, coming here alone, hunting you without the proper equipment. Well, lets get it over with then. I will not run from you nor beg for my life like a coward." He met the dragon's eyes coldly, even though his heart was pounding in his chest like a smith's hammer. The dragon shook his head slowly. "You just don't understand, do you, Boy? I don't WANT to kill you. All I've wanted for the last 150 years is to be left in peace." He stamped his foot angrily, the ground shaking, small pebbles falling from the wall onto Regan's head. "All I want is to be left alone until I die. Your people made it so I'm alone, isn't that enough? You took everything from me. My subjects.. my mate.. my children, all of them dead by human hands. I've watched you over the years, spreading further and further from the castle, settling lands we used to walk freely on. I never bothered ANY of you! Why can't you just leave a tired old dragon alone? Go rule your people or something. I'll pass to the next realm soon enough and you won't have to worry about it any more. I don't expect such will happen though, will it? You're going to run back to the castle and get the CORRECT arrows and then come back here with a larger party and finish the job your great grandfather started, aren't you?"

The great beast sighed deeply, nodding in acceptance. "Well, so be it, then. Go away, boy, go fetch your hunters and come back and kill me. Until then you're interrupting a perfectly good nap." Prince Regan studied the dragon closely for a moment. He took a deep breath, letting it out in a sigh. "You are their King, aren't you? The King of Dragonkind. I recognize your tone. You speak like my father does, and his father before him. I know a true leader when I speak with one."

The dragon nodded slowly. "I WAS the king of my kind, yes. Until my kind were no more. I imagine your father would sound much like I do if everyone who looked to him for help was wiped out and there was nothing he could do about it. Now go, Boy. Go away from me. Gather your troops and finish me off. I'm tired and I'm lonely. All I have is the other creatures of the forest to keep me company. "

He smiled slightly, great yellowish white fangs gleaming in the light. "Fine company they are, too, and I will miss them, but you have found me so it is time to go home." Prince Regan thought for a moment. Standing in front of him was the key to his future success. All he needed to do was go gather some hunters, get the great onyx arrows from their place of honor in the armory, come back and finish the great beast who stood before him now, wanting to die. He slowly shook his head negatively.

"On my honor I will not. No one will hear about our meeting, My Lord. You spared my life when I was too brash and stupid to know any better and now I shall spare yours. I would, however, like to return, to speak with you further. Apparently there was much missed in the stories I was told, and much I could learn from you, if you permit it."

The dragon nodded slowly, staring curiously at the young Prince. "If you wish, Young Prince. I will be here for as long as I am here. Farewell, until you return. I am going back to my nap. It is far to fine a day and the sun is to warm to remain awake for long." With that statement the dragon turned away, climbed back onto his rock without another word and promptly fell back asleep.

Chapter 6

Prince Regan was understandably shaken as he walked away from the hidden glade. He felt a strong desire for human companionship, but could not yet bring himself to return to the castle and all of the politics and posturing it required. He thought for a moment, remembering a small roadside inn not terribly far away. He had seen it once, long ago when he was returning back from a diplomatic trip to one of the outlying regions of the Kingdom. For some reason the place had always remained stuck in his head. He always intended to return there someday, but life had, as so often happens, gotten in the way.

As he got closer he stopped for a moment at a clear stream, looking at his reflection for a moment as he cleaned the grime of the trail from his body. "Well, not much likelihood I'll get a princely reception looking like this." He eyed his dust covered hunting clothes and three days growth of stubble in the slow ripples of the water.

"Perhaps its for the best, though. I really don't feel like being a Prince at the moment. I don't feel very princely anyway." He approached the inn, a modest log structure situated off the side of the road a bit, and he noticed with approval the tidiness of it all. A small garden in back to provide vegetables for the kitchen, a well maintained barn to hold their animals and a closely fitted cobblestone path bordered with small blue wildflowers led to the door. He paused for a moment and inhaled, his stomach rumbling from the scent of stew and baking bread, which filled the air.

He smiled as he opened the door and walked inside, squinting for a moment while his eyes adjusted to the dim interior, and began looking around curiously.

A plump, friendly looking woman with greying blonde hair smiled and greeted him warmly as he entered. "Hello, Good sir! Welcome to the Day's Ride Inn. What can we do for you today?" Regan smiled at the friendly commoner greeting, happy to not be recognized for who he was. "A table please, good lady. Food if you have it ready, a mug of strong, dark ale and likely a room for the night. I've been hunting for a few days and a bed under me would be much appreciated." She eyed him for a moment, noticing nothing unusual about him. She smiled and walked toward the common area, motioning him to follow. "Oh, I think we can take care of what you need here, Sir. The stew is fresh, the bread just finished baking and we have the richest ale and the softest beds in the realm, aside from the castle of course!"

He stiffened for a moment as she said that, afraid he'd been recognized, but then smiled as he recognized the humor in her tone. "Ah, very good! I'll take you up on all of them, then, since it's not likely I'll be sleeping in the castle any time soon." She showed him to a rough wooden table and he sat down, surveying the room. There were a few farmers sitting at the bar, talking with each other, a young couple with three children ringed around one of the larger tables, busily eating, and off in one of the dim corners was sitting.. he winced as he recognized two members of the royal guard sitting there, chatting with each other.

If they recognized him they would surely start posing and posturing, ruining his chance of blending in. He shifted a bit in his chair to better obscure his face from their view. "Is everything all right, Sir?" The woman asked in concern, noticing his reaction. "Hmmm? Oh, yes, yes.. everything is fine, Ma'am. Just not used to sitting in a chair like this. I developed a bit of a cramp as my legs stretched."

She nodded, not QUITE believing his story. "Ah. Well, then, I will have someone out shortly to bring your food to you, Sir." She turned away and he heard her as she walked into the kitchen. "Lucinda, would you take a bowl of stew, some bread and ale to the handsome gentleman at the corner table please? He's been out hunting and apparently he's half starved."

Regan sat back and relaxed, half closing his eyes, enjoying the sounds and smells of the inn. Soon the door opened and a girl walked out, carrying a tray heavy with his order. His breath caught in his throat as he saw her. She was beautiful. Her long, golden hair was tied back in a braid, revealing her high cheekbones, shining, emerald green eyes and her full red lips, which were right now parted in a slightly sarcastic smile. She set the tray of food on the table.

"Here you go, Sir. This should fill you up. You say you were out hunting?" He nodded, still stricken by her beauty. "How long were you out for?" He shook his head slightly, breaking the spell she had over him momentarily. "Um.. Three days, Miss."

She shook her head sympathetically. "Three days and you're starving. You must not have gotten any game then." He shook his head negatively. "No, I didn't get anything this time, Miss. It happens that way sometimes." She grinned mischievously as she turned away to head back to the kitchen. "Ah, you must not be a very good hunter then, Sir. Enjoy your meal!" He watched her walk away, his mouth open in surprise. No one had ever dared talk to him in such a manner! He tried to come up with a timely retort, but by the time he could think of anything to say more witty than "oh yeah?" she was already back in the kitchen.

He sighed and shrugged, then began eating some of the best stew and fresh bread he had ever tasted. Over the course of the night he saw her several more times. She chatted with him a bit longer each time she returned to refill his ale. After a time they exchanged names and he noticed her glancing over his way and smiling as she waited on the other customers. He didn't notice her raised eyebrow when he sighed in relief as the guards stood and went on their way.

Eventually he was the last one left in the common area, all others having come and gone. He was loathe to head to his bed and have the night come to an end, though, so he sat and drank slowly as the fire burned down to embers. Eventually she walked out once more. "Did you need anything else, Regan? We're about to close the kitchen for the night. You're welcome to sit here as long as you like, but I'm going to start cleaning if you don't mind."

He smiled and shook his head. "No, I'm fine, thank you. I'm just enjoying the company and I'm not quite ready to sleep yet." She blushed slightly at his compliment, smiling as she cleaned the dining area. He watched her work, finally working up the courage to ask her.

"Would you sit and chat with me a bit, Lucinda? It has been far to long since I've been able to enjoy the company of such a pretty girl." She paused briefly to consider and then smiled and set down the bucket and brush she had been using to clean the tables. She moved over and sat across from him. "I'd like that, but I can't stay long, I'm afraid. I have to be up with the chickens to get ready for breakfast. We always get a passel of starving hunters who want their eggs and porridge in the morning." She winked at him, taking the sting out of the little dig at his expense. They chatted then, ending up talking for hours about nothing.

As they talked the Prince grew more and more fascinated with the girl. She was smart and funny, fiercely independent, not like the girls at court at all. She actually had opinions about things and was not afraid to share them with him. They discussed politics and at times Regan had to bite his tongue when she mentioned unfair taxes or the Prince, sitting up in his castle not understanding what things are like for REAL people. He asked about the meat in the stew and she told him they bought it from poachers who hunted the area because that was the only way they could afford a steady supply of meat. Finally she stopped talking and looked deeply into his eyes. She decided to ask him what had been bothering her a bit all night.

"Regan? Why were you afraid of those guardsmen that were here earlier? Are you a criminal? Both Mother and I noticed your reaction toward them."

He blinked twice, shocked at the directness of the question. His mouth opened and closed, trying to form words. Finally he started laughing. Once he started he couldn't seem to stop. He laughed until tears rolled from his eyes. Lucinda watched him curiously, slightly afraid of his reaction. Had she been spending all this time with a madman?

Finally, once he could control himself once more he shook his head negatively. "No, Lucinda, I assure you, I'm no criminal." She eyed him doubtfully. "Well, what is it then? You just don't like guardsmen?" He looked at her for a long moment, trying to make up his mind. Finally he decided he liked her enough to tell her the truth.

"Lucinda.." He began slowly. "Do you know what the Prince's name is?" She rolled her eyes in annoyance at the ridiculousness of the question. "Of course I do, you silly man. Everyone does. It's Prince Re..." She stopped suddenly, her eyes widening in shock. "Oh! Oh.. oh no! You aren't! You.. You CAN'T be!" He smiled at her and nodded slowly. "Ah, but I'm afraid I am."

Her face showed an expression of horror as she remembered everything she had said. She had told him enough to not only get herself hung, but her family as well as the poachers. "Oh.. I am SO sorry My Lord! Please.. Forgive me for my stupidity!"

She stood immediately, curtsying deeply in front of him. It was his turn to roll his eyes this time. "Oh, would you please stop? Sit down, Lucinda. See? This is why I didn't want anyone to know who I was." He offered his hand across the table as she sat back down. She reached for it hesitantly and he enfolded her hand with his gently. He started speaking slowly.

"Being who I am, I don't have any real friends. Everyone poses and postures and tells me what they think I want to hear. You didn't do that, though. We talked and laughed and you were honest and real. You don't need to worry about the things you told me about. I respect your opinions and I would like to know more. Someday I have to rule this land and I would like to know what REAL people think of me."

He smiled a bit sarcastically as he said it. He took a deep breath and continued. "I like you, Lucinda. A lot. I would very much enjoy seeing you again if you would permit it."

She smiled at him, squeezing his hand lightly in return. "Well, I must admit, I DID like you quite a bit before I knew you were the Prince. I SUPPOSE I can get over the fact you're royalty. Only;; if you don't tell anyone else, though. I wouldn't want my friends all making fun of me for seeing you."

He laughed, nodding. "I agree. I think we should keep our little secret as well. I mean, I would hate to embarrass you." She smiled as she looked deeply into his eyes, her own green ones gleaming in the light from the fire. "You still aren't a very good hunter, though. You're going to have to work on it."

He stared into her eyes and nodded. "I have to say, Right now I'm glad I'm not a very good hunter. If my belly had been full I may never have stopped for the night."

Chapter 7

Although Lucinda's mother had told the truth, the bed at the inn Regan slept in during night was quite nearly as soft as his own at the castle, sleep did not come easily to him. He lay awake for a long time, his thoughts bouncing between the fact he had not only met a real live dragon, but possibly the girl he had been searching for all his life as well. He smiled to himself in the darkness.

"Of course, both of them are going to complicate my life beyond imagining." Finally, late into the night he fell into a restless slumber.

The next morning he was awake at first light. He dressed quickly and went down the stairs to the common room, looking around eagerly to see Lucinda again. Soon she arrived, breezing into the room, looking as though she had slept for a month. Her hair was once again braided tightly, her face was freshly scrubbed and she had the same wide, slightly sarcastic grin on her face from the night before. "About time you woke up, Regan! I've been up for the last two hours, getting ready to feed the hungry hordes."

He looked at her in surprise just before her mother walked by, slapping her playfully on the arm. "LUCINDA! Don't you lie to that boy! You know very well I had to threaten to dump a bucket of cold water over your head to get you out of bed this morning! I can't imagine what you were doing up so late. It's never taken you so long to finish your chores before."

With a wink at Regan the woman continued past the two of them, heading into the kitchen to check on the morning's bread. Lucinda grinned at him sheepishly. "Well, I guess you caught me!" She giggled then, but unlike the grating, forced noises the girls at the castle made, hers was pleasant, full of life and fun. He smiled at her like the village idiot, amazed by her.

She took him by the arm and led him to a table, quickly bringing a platter of food laden with steaming eggs and smoked meat, thick porridge and fresh bread. He realized how hungry he was as he took in the sight of the food and he dug into it eagerly, devouring most of it before sitting back with a satisfied sigh.

Once the breakfast crowd had come and gone for the day she came and sat with him again for a bit. "Well, Regan, How is this country lifestyle agreeing with you?" She took a quick glance around to make sure no one was within listening distance. "Ready to head back to your nice, soft castle life yet?"

He smiled and shook his head. "Lucinda, I would gladly spend every day like this. If I had a choice I would never go back there."

She raised an eyebrow in surprise. "Really? I always imagined life as the Prince would be a living dream. You don't have to do anything you don't want to, you have servants to do everything for you, there is always plenty of food, how could it possibly be so bad?"

He chuckled and shook his head. "I guess I never looked at it like that. Every moment of every day I'm there is planned out and scheduled for me. I have to smile and nod at some of the most odious people you can imagine, I can't get friendly with the servants because they are always worried about saying something that might offend me. I live in a very pretty cage, Lucinda, fed, bathed and watered like a prized pet. "

She snorted mockingly. "A prized pet who can have someone hanged on a whim." He looked at her for a moment, reaching out and taking her hand in his own.

"Would you walk with me for a bit? As much as I love the atmosphere in here, I long to be out in the forest."

She paused for a moment, hesitantly. "Well.. I would have to ask my father. Perhaps I could go for a short walk with you, just until lunch time." He nodded and they stood, walking out of the inn. She led him around back to where her father was cutting wood.

The muscular, graying man stopped working as they approached, wiping his gleaming brow with a cloth. He eyed the couple, his mouth twisted into a teasing grin.

"Well, who do we have here? You must be the reason Lucinda decided to stay up with the owls last night, eh?" Lucinda blushed as Regan bowed to the man.

"My apologies, Sir. I didn't mean to keep her up so late. We were talking and time simply flew by." He offered his hand. "I'm Regan."

The man took his hand in his own calloused one. "Connor. It's good to meet you, Regan. Now, what can I do for the two of you today?" Regan paused, not entirely sure how to proceed. Typically men were all but throwing their daughters at him. He had never had to ask permission to go for a walk with one before. "Well, Sir, I was wondering if you could spare your daughter for a bit. Only for an hour or so, to go for a walk with me."

The large man stood for a moment, looking deeply into Regan's eyes, sizing him up carefully. "Well.." He replied slowly. "Are your intentions honorable, Boy?" Regan nodded emphatically.

"Oh, most definitely, Sir. I would just like a chance to continue my conversation with your daughter." The man nodded, apparently satisfied.

"Go then, but you best be back before the lunch crowd gets here, Lucinda." She grinned and nodded. "I will, Father, I promise!" She looked over at Regan. "Just let me get my cloak, I'll be right back!" She turned and ran to the house, leaving the two men alone for a moment.

Connor's expression darkened a bit and he stared at Regan ominously. "Just remember, Boy, Prince or not, if you touch my daughter in anything less than an honorable way, I'll split your head like cordwood and feed you to the hogs." Regan stood, shocked. His jaw fell open in surprise.

"How.. how do you know who I am, Sir?" The man chuckled and shrugged before turning back to his chopping. "I saw you and your father when you were at the harvest festival last year. It was my mead you awarded first prize to. I remember you asked your father to award me with the contract to provide the mead for the castle. He muttered something about not offending the brewer's guild and the two of you moved on. "

Regan nodded, grinning widely. "Ah yes, I remember now! Best mead I ever tasted, Sir!" Connor bowed deeply, obviously honored by the statement. "Well, thank you kindly, Prince. There will be a case of it waiting for you at the castle when you decide to return there." He winked, splitting a log effortlessly. "Just don't tell your royal brewers or your father, I wouldn't want to offend anyone!"

Lucinda appeared outside, her cloak wrapped around her shoulders, and gave her father an impatient look.

He chuckled and nodded in her direction. "You better go, M'Lord. I don't think either of us wants to be responsible for keeping this one waiting. Just mind what I told you." With that he turned and went back to cutting wood, a large, round log splitting effortlessly under his axe.

Chapter 8

The two of them walked for a while, neither of them saying much, just enjoying the bright morning sunshine and the sights and smells of the forest around them. Soon they found what was left of an old cobblestone path and began to follow it. Prince Regan looked over at Lucinda.

"Did you know your father recognized me?" She laughed and shook her head. "No, I didn't, but it doesn't surprise me. He talked for months about what you said about his mead. Told everyone who walked in the door about it."

Regan chuckled. "Well, It was good mead. If I would have known what a beautiful daughter he had I would have made sure his beer won first prize, too." He grinned playfully as she punched him lightly on the shoulder.

"See? That's exactly what I mean, Regan! You speak and others do exactly what you want them to. You don't have to live by the rules the rest of us do."

He let out a short, mocking laugh. "Ah, how little you know of castle life, my dear. Do you know the night before I came on this trip I was chastised by my father for pouring my own wine because I made the wine steward look bad? I have to live by a million and one rules, and I'm afraid I'm not very good at any of them."

He sighed, suddenly sober. "I'm don't think I will be a very good King. In fact, if I weren't the Prince, and his only son, I'm fairly sure I would have been kicked out of court by now."

She looked over at him with a sparkle in her eyes. Suddenly she leaned up and kissed him on the cheek. "Its okay, Regan. If they decide to chase you out you can always come out here and be a hunter. Well, if you ever learn to get any game, that is." She laughed as he reached up and rubbed his cheek in surprise. He opened his mouth to reply when suddenly he stopped, looking off into the forest.

"Lucinda! Look!" She turned and gasped as she saw it, the ruins of what once must have been a beautiful castle, dull grey in the late morning sun. The stones lay about from the crumbled towers, lichen and moss growing thick over them. Some of the archways still stood, the mysterious shadows beckoning them, begging for exploration.

They walked over to it slowly, awestruck. Neither of them realized their hands instinctively sought the other's, each one gripping the other hand tightly as they walked into the ruins, looking around in amazement.

Finally Regan spoke, in an awed voice. "This must be the castle of the old ones! I've read about them in some of the old books at home. No one has been able to find this place for centuries!"

Lucinda looked around for a moment, speechless. "But.. this has never been here before! I've walked all over these woods. Surely I would have found it before now." Suddenly Regan remembered something and gasped. "The prophecy!" He exclaimed. "Lucinda.. I'm going to have to leave for a while when we get back. I need to go speak to someone."

She looked at him curiously. "What prophecy are you talking about, Regan? You have to leave? I don't understand.." He took a deep breath and began slowly. "Well, I read it in one of the oldest books at the castle. I didn't understand it at the time. I don't remember all of it, but the first part said, 'And Mhirachor shall reappear when dragons and men live as one once more, and magic will return to the land." She shook her head, looking at him as if her were insane. "Dragons? Regan, there hasn't been a dragon around in a hundred years! Your Great grandfather wiped them from the land." He smiled and shook his head. "No, we only THOUGHT he did. In fact, I happened to meet one yesterday.

The Dragon King

That's who I must go speak to."

She looked at him doubtfully. "A dragon? You met a DRAGON yesterday? And you spoke with him?" She sighed and shook her head. "Why is it all the cute princes are lunatics?"

He gripped her shoulders and turned her to look at him. He stared deeply into her eyes, silently begging her to believe him. "Lucinda, I swear to you. It's the truth. I found his tracks and followed him back to his lair. I was going to kill him to take his head back home to legitimize my claim to the throne. I had forgotten you needed onyx arrows to hurt them. He could have killed me, but instead we talked."

She returned his gaze, seeing how badly he wanted to be believed. She made up her mind then, seeing the desperation in his gaze. "Regan, if you say you spoke with a dragon, I believe you. Even if we weren't standing in the courtyard of a castle that disappeared 500 years ago, I would still believe you. Maybe I'm as mad as you are, but I think you're telling me the truth. If you need to go, then go. I only ask you return soon to let me know that you're all right."

She smiled up at him, her expression erasing all his doubts and fears somehow. "For some reason, despite all of the logic screaming in my head, I've grown quite fond of you over the time we've spent together. I know we can never be together, Regan. I understand that you would never be allowed to marry a common girl, but I'm afraid I've developed some feelings for you anyway. You are going to make some royal painted trollop a fine husband, and I will be proud to call you my King."

He kissed her then, in the courtyard, with all of the spirits of the ancients looking down on them.

Chapter 9

Araseth sat for a long time after Regan left. The sun baked down on him warmly, but he could not fall asleep. Seeing the young Prince had brought up many emotions he thought he had put behind him long ago.

The rage he felt when he realized who the young human was nearly made him lose control. Before he was able to stop himself he nearly bit the young human in half. The scent of him, so like his ancestor, the bow pointed at his face. He shuddered as he thought about how close he had come to losing control. The ancestor of the man who had murdered his mate and younglings stood in front of him and he took no revenge. He talked to him instead. Even though he knew it was the right thing to do it had been so very hard..

As he lazed in the sun the visions of that horrible day returned to him, playing over and over in his mind. He heard again the cries of terror from his younglings as they were slaughtered, heard his mate's voice begging for mercy. He saw the look of pure hatred on the hunters' faces as they drove their onyx tipped spears into the one he loved with all his heart and spirit.

He shuddered at the visions, gasping for breath as he felt the fire in his side once more, his scales tearing from his body as the horrible arrow pierced his side. Finally he opened his eyes and spoke to the air.

"I let him live because of you, Adelind. Knowing you wouldn't approve is the only reason I didn't kill the boy. I know it wouldn't bring you back to me and you would be saddened by my actions if you were watching me. I miss you, my beloved. Everything good I am is because of you."

He closed his eyes and finally drifted into a restless sleep. Soon dark approached, and with it his friends, the creatures of the forest. He opened his eyes and saw the fairies and sprites, the deer standing proudly behind them, the squirrels high up in the rocks, all chattering to each other impatiently, waiting for their stories.

He smiled at them, at once glad for their company and yet, at the same time, not being able to bear their presence.

"No stories tonight I'm afraid, my friends." He rumbled. They all sighed and muttered in disappointment. "Seeing the young Prince today has put me off a bit, I'm afraid. Perhaps I will be more in the mood tomorrow night."

With that said he stood and stretched his wings to the night sky. With a mighty flap he rose from the ground, rising through the air until he settled at last on the very top of the highest mountain.

He settled there, gazing down at the castle far below, watching the flickering lights of the village as the humans went about their lives. His breath made great billowing clouds in the frigid night air.

"So small they all look from up here." He mused. "How could such tiny, insignificant creatures have destroyed our race?"

He sighed once more, remembering how he and Adelind used to come here on nights such as this. They watched the magical colored lights dance in the sky for hours, never speaking. Being next to each other was enough.

Now she was gone forever and he was left here, a mere shell of what he once was. The lights in the sky seemed to taunt him tonight, making him feel more alone than he had in a very long time. The memories of his beloved mate, seeing the young Prince, thinking about how much he had lost in this life became almost too much for him to stand once more.

Finally he looked down at the jagged rocks far below him. How easy it would be, he thought. A little jump, tuck the wings to my side, a moment of falling and then.. Nothing.

He sighed once more, shaking his head. "But that is a cowards way. For some reason my life was spared on that day. The Great Spirits have a plan for me, which has not been revealed yet. There is a reason I continue to live, and so I will continue to live until I don't live any longer, for that is my destiny. To do any less would be an insult and an unforgivable breech of faith to all who ever counted on me."

Making that decision, he looked away from the jagged rocks below and instead looked upward into the night sky for a long time, watching the stars shift and change as they made their way across the sky, the dancing, magical lights swirling and pulsating, once becoming the deep, glowing green of his beloved mate's eyes.

He smiled when he saw that, and for a moment he felt that his Adelind was beside him, that the steam of her breath billowed in the air next to him, and mixed with his own. He could feel her side pressed against his for the briefest of moments and for a fleeting instant he was happy once more.

The Dragon King

Chapter 10

Regan looked back longingly over his shoulder as he headed down the road away from the inn. He realized that there was no place he would rather be than back there, sitting at a table and talking with Lucinda.

He sighed, knowing that they would never be together since she was not of royal blood. Soon he was off the road and back in the woods once more, where he had been the most comfortable before. Now, though, the forest didn't seem quite as welcoming as it had.

After several hours he found the trail between the rock walls again. He slipped between the two guardian walls and moved down the pathway, the shadows of the day growing long as he walked. He emerged into the clearing once more and quickly spotted the dragon laying in the same spot he had been when Prince Regan had last seen him. The sun had moved away from his reclining body and he was just starting to sit up, blinking his great green eyes after his afternoon nap.

He spotted the Prince almost instantly, his long, serpentine neck snaking around so he could look at the Prince. "Back so soon?" he asked, in his soft, rumbling voice. He raised an eyebrow as he looked around curiously. "I don't see any hunters escorting you. Are you foolish enough to try to kill me again by yourself?"

Regan looked the massive beast over for a moment, swallowing nervously as he approached closer. "I gave you my word, Dragon. I have no intention of killing you. I am simply here to speak with you." The dragon stared at him for a moment, holding the human's gaze with his own inhuman one. "That truly is a pity." He said simply before looking away. The Prince approached closer, curiosity twisting his brow a bit. "You WANT me to kill you, Dragon?" The monster sighed and shrugged, his great wings rustling a bit.

"Prince Regan, I quite honestly don't care if you kill me, if I die of old age or if a rock falls and crushes my skull to powder. I find myself caring about very little these days, and explaining myself to an infant human who had the pure blind luck of finding me interests me not at all. If I had my way you would turn around, leave and never show yourself to me again. However, if you insist on speaking to me, my name is Araseth, not dragon."

Regan shook his head, surprised and a bit angered by the great beast's words. "Well, then. Maybe I SHOULD have gone and gotten the onyx arrows from the castle, Araseth. Putting your head on display would certainly remove any objections from those who don't exactly love me have about me ascending the throne. I must ask before I go retrieve the devices of your demise, though, why do you want to die so badly?"

Araseth's eyes narrowed dangerously at the Prince's words, thin plumes of smoke rising from his nostrils as he stared at the Prince.

"I think, young Prince," He spat, venomously, " A more appropriate question would be why would I want to live? All I once had has been taken from me by your ancestor's hand, if you recall. I hide myself to live and I have no one to love anymore. I can't even go swim without fear that someone may see me and there will be hoards of hunters hounding me to try to finish the job once more."

He stared at Regan coldly. "Would YOU want to live like that for a few hundred years, Prince? Would you enjoy your life if you saw the deaths of every person you ever cared about replayed over and over again in your head every single time you closed your eyes to sleep?" Regan broke eye contact with the angry beast. He lowered his head in shame and shook it.

"No," he said softly, "I would not. Were I in your place I would likely have thrown myself off the highest mountain I could find by now, merely to end that pain."

Araseth chuckled then, softly. It sounded like the rustle of dry leaves through the trees and Prince Regan looked up at him, confused.

"Then you and I are much alike, Prince. I can't count the number of times I have considered doing that very thing. There are two things in the world that stop me. Among dragons it is said that if you take your own life you never get to pass through the veil into the next world. You will be cursed to wander forever, a shadow on the land, nothing more. This fact doesn't bother me much. However, if I were to do that and lost the only chance I have of ever seeing Adelind and my young once more I would never forgive myself. That, and I believe I was spared for a reason that day that I as yet do not understand. The Spirits did not want me to die and so I lived. For what purpose I do not know, I merely know my story in this realm is not finished yet. And that is why I have not done it."

Regan looked up at the dragon and nodded in understanding. "That's why you want me to end your life, then. A mercy killing and a fitting end to your story." He sighed and shook his head. "It would make me happy to be able to honor your wishes for such a good reason, Araseth, but I think it may be a while yet before it is your time to go to your rest. It seems there may be many more chapters of the story of your life yet to be written. Mhirachor has reappeared once again."

The dragon gasped in surprise, eyes widening as he shook his head negatively. "Mhirachor? Not possible, boy.

The castle of the old ones disappeared before I was even hatched! It has been gone since the Separation!"

Regan looked confused at that. Araseth shook his head impatiently. "Surely you know about the Separation? You must have records of it?" Regan shook his head negatively. "I only found one reference to Mhirachor, and it was in the oldest volume in the castle. The books we have apparently don't go back far enough to speak about any separation. What was it exactly?"

The dragon shook his head in wonder, a faint smile on his face. He gestured to a flat rock. "Sit, Boy." He rumbled. "My friends will be here soon and I will tell that story tonight. The most important story you have ever heard. I will tell you about how dragons and men parted ways, back in the old times."

He raised an eyebrow and held Regan in his gaze. "Are you sure you want to hear this, Boy? I will tell the story from the Dragon's perspective. It will not always favor your relatives."

The Prince moved over to the rock and sat down, incredulous. "You know of the old ones, then?" He asked, awed. "No man left alive has any knowledge of who they were or what happened to them."

He considered for a moment, then finally nodded. "I would prefer to hear the story from your perspective, Araseth. I realize that every story has many sides to it, depending on who is telling it. As the future King of my people I would be remiss to think that knowing only one side of the account told me the truth of it."

The dragon cocked his head slightly, finally nodding in approval. "As you wish, then. You shall hear the story." Regan thought he saw a flicker out of the corner of his eye, but he dismissed it as a trick of the light. He nodded excitedly. "This information is amazing! I wish the court historian were here to hear it!"

He glanced down then, after feeling something bump lightly against his knee. He thought perhaps an errant beetle had landed on him and went to brush it away when he gasped, loudly. A tiny girl, perfectly formed and no bigger than a mouse, wearing a tiny, shimmering purple tunic, sat cross-legged on his knee.

She looked up at him and smiled, waving up at him, her translucent wings quivering a bit, glowing slightly as the last light of the day faded. Araseth chuckled as he noticed Regan's shocked expression.

"One of my friends." He explained, looking around. "Here come the others now." Regan looked around and saw hundreds of tiny flickering lights making their way into the valley, settling in nooks and crevices on the high walls, one or two fluttering up to Araseth and kissing him on his nose before settling in. Regan heard a soft buzz in his ear and glanced over, one of them landing lightly on his shoulder. "Faeries?" he gasped in shock. "But.. Faeries aren't real! They are something out of children's stories!"

The tiny girl on his shoulder in the pink dress frowned up at him, shaking her fist in his direction. Araseth actually laughed at her actions, shaking his head. "No, Regan, I assure you, they are quite real. Humans don't see them anymore because they don't want to be seen. Also because magic is not nearly as strong in the world anymore so it is hard for them to be visible. Here it is easy for them, they feed off of the magic that dissipates from me."

He eyed the several faeries that had settled on Regan. He now had one on each shoulder, one on each knee, and one sitting, precariously balanced on his head. "I must say, Regan, I am surprised. Faeries generally don't get close to humans. You really must be something special. But- the hour grows late, so let us begin our story for the evening." Araseth's eyes glowed a bright green for a moment and then Regan gasped in surprise once more as the sky above the dragon's head began getting lighter.

Soon figures could be seen plainly, moving about and speaking to each other as the Dragon's voice began speaking softly. "Many years ago, before I was even hatched, Humans and Dragons fought together to chase the dark ones from our world.

The ogres and giants and other dark creatures from the otherworld had come here to take this land as their own. The fighting was brutal and it lasted for many years, longer than the span of a Dragon's life even. Humans and dragons and Faeries all banded together, working as a single unit to fight the beasts back into the darkness that they came from, but they were losing the battle."

Regan sat, spellbound, watching the characters play out the battle scenes above Araseth's head, the groups of humans fighting bravely, the dragons screaming down out of the clouds, raking fiercely at the horrible monsters in the vision. Faeries darted among the dark forces, blinding their opponents as the humans wove amongst them, flailing clubs wildly, breaking knees and elbows and heads, whatever they were able to strike.

The dragon continued the story. "Whenever darkness fell, the creatures grew stronger. They could only be defeated in the light of day. All of the races of the world worked together tirelessly, but until they invented a way to have light in the darkness, they were doomed to fail. One day an ancestor of mine discovered something. She created fire. The flames that she made grew bright and hot, and chased the creatures of the darkness away.

Once she had discovered this and how to create it, she shared it willingly with all the creatures of the world. Again, all worked together and, since the creatures were no longer able to have such an advantage at night, the war was eventually won."

Prince Regan smiled, watching the scene above, men and women and dragons all dancing together around a huge fire while the faeries darted around amongst their heads happily, dipping and weaving and playing.

"The days after the dark ones were defeated were wondrous indeed." Araseth spoke, his voice drawing Regan into the story once again. "Many wonderful things were discovered after fire was invented. Over the centuries man discovered steel, and weapons improved. Homes and castles were built, crops were raised and shared among all. The faerie folk taught the humans how to be one with nature, how to plant and grow food and how to use the trees to build their shelters.

The Dragons watched man proudly as they grew stronger and prospered and advanced. All worked together tirelessly for the good of everyone in the land. Truly, these creatures were our brothers. Although they didn't look like us, they fought with the ferocity of dragonkind."

Prince Regan watched the scene above the dragon's head, the brutish, furry men clad only in furs progressing, advancing, building houses and growing crops, always with the dragons and faeries by their side.

"The dark ones were not gone forever however," Araseth continued his narrative. "After many hundreds of years the humans let them back into the light once more. They were mining for ore when they accidentally broke through one of the long buried gateways, freeing the monsters to come into our lands once again. This time the monsters knew what they would be facing and they had hundreds of years to prepare as well.

When they came boiling through the gateway all of this world's forces gathered once more, the sacred fire ready to repel them again. This time, though, the fire did not work. The creatures had discovered fire of their own, and learned how to defend against it. Some died, but it was not nearly as effective as before and soon, another great war broke out and once again the combined forces of this world were losing."

More great battle scenes appeared, this time with humans wearing armor, riding the dragons into battle as archers stood in the background, raining arrows down on the dark forces.

"Our most intelligent dragons, faeries and humans went back to work, desperately trying to find something that would win the day once more. After many hundreds of years the dragons were successful again and my ancestors discovered the force that we now call magic. It came easily to dragons and faeries, merging quickly with our spirits and becoming part of us. It was not so easy for humans, though. They had great difficulty understanding and wielding that power. Their spirits were simply not ready for it yet. And so, the dragon and the faerie used these new magical powers against the monsters."

Suddenly the pictures changed, the dragons blasting fire from their mouths, huge rocks and storms flailing against the forces of darkness, lightning striking them mercilessly. Sparkling lights danced from the faerie folk now, their tiny gleaming barbed daggers striking the dark creatures and wounding them, leaving them as easy targets for the humans to finish them. Slowly they retreated back into the mountain that they came from.

"After years of incessant fighting, we again won the day. The evil forces were beaten back into the mountain and using magic we sealed the gateway once more." The scene shifted again, showing an entire mountainside erupting into a volcano, the lava flowing over the mouth of the cave, sealing it. "Again, all races rejoiced. For many years after we all lived in peace once more as dragons and faeries helped the humans rebuild all they had lost. In gratitude the humans built Mhirachor, the castle of the Dragon, a place where all races of the world were welcome to gather and celebrate." The picture shifted, showing the great high walls and delicate archways and towers of the ruin that Regan and Lucinda had discovered. Araseth sighed.

"Soon after that, though, things began to change, as all things must in time. The humans asked the dragons for this wonderful magic they had discovered. Their reasoning was, since the dragons had given them fire they should do the same with magic. The elder dragons refused, however. They said that humans weren't ready for magic yet, that the forces that it called forth were far too powerful, too dangerous to all the creatures that lived in the world. The humans grew angry, pouting like petulant children. 'You just want to keep the power for yourselves!' They cried. "With your magic you could rule us! You could make us your slaves, just as the dark ones wanted to.' Still the elders refused, saying that the humans were not ready for that responsibility yet.

In time, perhaps,, but not now. Eventually a few humans managed to discover the secret. Not all of the magic, but a bit of it, and they grew powerful compared to the others. Humans rallied to their new, more powerful leaders and soon there was fighting among them.

They spoke with the dragons less and less and none went to Mhirachor any longer. The days of peace and brotherhood had left the land.

Humans went their separate ways as well. Kingdoms were formed, armies raised. Eventually the strongest of them decided to declare war on our kind, hoping to win the entire secret of our powers, which were still much greater than theirs. Although it saddened us, the dragons had no choice but to strike back and kill the King of that land and lay waste to their Kingdom. After the war was over the dragons and the humans and the faerie went one last time to

Mhirachor, to discuss how we were going to live in the same world after all that had happened.

It was agreed that we would all go our separate ways in the world. The humans declared that contact with our kind and with the faeries, who had sided with us in the battle, would be broken off and we were no longer welcome in their settlements.

As a sign of this agreement Mhirachor was to be destroyed, the symbol of peace and brotherhood removed from the land just as the feelings we once had for each other were removed from our minds. One human stood up after the decision was made, however."

Regan felt the dragon's eyes staring at him and he wiggled uncomfortably under the gaze. "Conall was his name. Not your Great Grandfather, Regan, but his namesake. He was a king of your people from many generations past. He stood and he pleaded with the assembly to reconsider.

He claimed that there was still hope. When all turned a deaf ear to him he asked if he could be granted one favor. He asked that Mhirachor be sent away, sent into the void until a time when all species could once again unite. Until everyone could make things as they were once again. Only then would the old castle re-appear to usher in the new age of peace and prosperity among all races.

His favor was eventually granted, although most said that the castle would never again show itself on the lands of this world. That was the Separation. That was when our kinds all went their own way in the world."

The images faded then, the figures blurring and finally disappearing into smoke as all of the faeries clapped wildly, rising into the air and buzzing about happily before finally making their way down the trail once more. Regan blinked in surprise as the one who had been sitting on his knee fluttered up and placed a feather light kiss on his nose before she went on her way. Araseth chuckled.

"I think Marimo likes you." Prince Ragan sat for a moment, thinking.

"But, Mhirachor has reappeared, Araseth. What does that mean? How could dragons and humans ever unite again? We wiped your kin from the earth, except for you."

Araseth grinned, his gleaming fangs shining in the light of the full moon overhead. "You humans think you know everything, do you not? Have you ever considered that one dragon escaped you, perhaps there were others as well? There are not many of us, Prince, but a few remain. I sent them away from here, to all the corners of the world to avoid having them slain like their kin. I haven't seen them in a very long time, but they live still. I feel a fierce pain in my spirit when one of my kind passes into the next realm and I have thankfully not felt that for many years.

As for Mhirachor reappearing, I cannot tell you why. Perhaps the magic just failed after so long a time. I hope you enjoyed the Telling of the Story, Regan. It is very late now and I must sneak out to find something to feed on before the light of day comes once more. Feel free to find a soft patch of moss to roll your bed onto. No harm will befall you while you rest here. You are under my protection."

With that said the great dragon stood and flapped his wings, rising into the air. Regan watched the deep shadow rise from the canyon and sail into the night. He unrolled his bedding slowly, carefully replaying the story he had been told in his mind.

Chapter 11

For a time things fell into a strange sort of a pattern for Prince Regan. He divided his time between talking with Araseth and travelling back to the inn to see Lucinda.

He took to hunting as he travelled back and forth, always making sure to bring wild venison or boar to the inn when he arrived. He would grin and wink at Lucinda as he carried the day's catch into the kitchen, dropping it on the large wooden table with a solid 'thump'. He then turned to her proudly asking, "Well? How is this, Lucinda? Am I a better hunter yet?"

She would walk over and look the game over critically for a moment. "Well.. it IS a bit small. You must have only been able to shoot the runt of the litter. Still, I guess its better than nothing." She would smirk and look into his eyes, stealing a quick kiss from him the moment they were alone.

He was quite amused one day when Lucinda's mother took him to the side and whispered to him while her daughter was busy serving the other guests. "Regan," She admonished quietly. "Although we appreciate all the game you've been bringing us, you really must stop! The King's guardsmen have been around a lot lately, and they aren't kind when they catch a poacher in the King's forest! I would hate to see you get in trouble. Lucinda has grown very fond of you, and it would break her heart to see you thrown in the dungeons!"

Regan smiled at her words, placing a comforting hand on her shoulder. "Don't you worry about a thing, Mamai. I promise, the Kings guards won't catch me. I'm MUCH to quick for them!" She hmphed indignantly and shook her head. "Ah, youth! No one can catch you, can they? Just wait until you're older, Regan! Then you'll see that we're not so invulnerable, you and I!"

She stopped speaking suddenly and looked at Regan pleadingly. "Just you make sure you don't hurt Lucinda. She's all we've got. Someday this place will be hers, you know. I hope she has a good, strong man around to help her run it!" She smiled and winked at Prince Regan then and swept off to attend to something in the kitchen.

She meant for the comment to be amusing, but it tore a hole in Regan's heart to hear her say it. He knew then that Lucinda's feelings for him had grown as fast and as strong as his own had for her.

He caught her as the crowd cleared that night. "Lucinda," he started to speak, the words swelling in his throat. "Lucinda, will you walk with me? I must speak to you." She looked around at the tables yet to be cleared and started to refuse, but something in his tone told her it was important. "Let me get my cloak." She said softly.

They walked together that night, the full, bright moon lighting the path with a silvery glow as they strolled toward the old castle. Neither said a word, both knowing what was about to be said. They walked in silence, holding hands in the quiet night.

When they reached the crumbling ruins they sat on an old bridge and watched the tiny fish flicker through the pools of moonlight. Finally she spoke, softly.

"You're leaving, aren't you?"

He sighed and nodded. "I am. What we are.. what I am doing to you. It isn't fair. You shouldn't be wasting your time with me, Lucinda. You should find a man you can love and be with forever."

She took his hand, squeezing it gently. She turned and looked at him for a long moment. The light of the moon bathed his face, washing the color from it until he looked like a statue, frozen in time.

"Regan. I found the man I will love for all time. You leaving is not going to change that. I know we can't be together. I've always known that, and yet I fell in love with you anyway. If you must leave, I understand. I know you need to go home, to get back to rule the Kingdom, but you'll always be here."

She took his hand and placed it on her chest, then smiled at him. He kissed her softly and sighed. "I wish things were different, Lucinda. I wish that I could take you with me back to the castle. I know Father would love you."

He grinned widely. "And I would give all my wealth to see you tear into the ladies of the court!" She slapped him gently on the arm, giggling.

"I'm going to leave at first light, Lucinda." He said, suddenly serious once more. "I'm going to go see Araseth for a while longer before I go home. I'm learning so much from him, so much of the history of our people that has been forgotten or just not written down. I feel like maybe if I spend some time with him some of his.. Kingliness might wear off on me."

He sighed. "It seems like the more I learn about being a King, the less I feel like I was ever born to be one."

She shook her head at him, a small smile on her lips. "Regan, you are one of the greatest men I have ever known." She said softly. "I just hope one of these days you realize that. You worry too much about ceremonies and traditions and whether you're going to do it correctly. Be yourself and the people will follow you. Respect them and they will love you. Father does, and he doesn't respect many people. I mean, I know I'm only the simple daughter of inn keepers, but it seems to me that when you own the playing field you're allowed to change the rules."

He smiled and shook his head in wonderment, leaning down and kissing her once more. "You never cease to amaze me, Lucinda. I've never known anyone like you before." He stood and helped her rise, holding her hand even after she stood. She smiled up at him, eyes twinkling in the moonlight, that sarcastic half grin on her lips that he had grown to love so much.

"Good! I'm glad that you have never met anyone like me before, Prince. That way I can reside alone in your heart. I DO hate crowds, you know."

The next morning he packed quickly and took a last look around the inn. He smiled and waved to some of the regular customers that he had grown to know over the weeks that he had stayed there. Rupert, one of the farmers from the area, gave him a wide grin and a knowing wink. "Your girl is in the kitchen, Regan. I think she might of cooked up somethin SPECIAL for you this morning, if'n you know what I mean!"

All of the men at the table burst out laughing, each encouraging Regan to go and 'see his Lady Love' He grinned, waving them off, hiding the strange melancholy he felt at the thought of not seeing them again.

He walked into the kitchen and looked around. Lucinda was there, a large bag of food waiting for him on the wooden table where he had thrown so much game. She turned quickly from him as he entered, wiping her eyes deftly with the back of her hand. She turned back to him, forcing a smile. "I made you some food for the road, Regan."

He walked over to her and wrapped his arms around her tightly, leaning down and whispering softly into her ear. "I love you, Lucinda."

Just then her mother and father walked into the kitchen, looking curiously at the large bag of food. Mamai looked between it and Regan for a long moment. "You're leaving then?" She asked softly.

He nodded. "I'm afraid so, Mamai. I need to attend to some pressing duties. I was just telling Lucinda good bye." The woman's eyes narrowed angrily. "This is because of that talk we had yesterday, isn't it? I hinted at marriage and you're running away scared, is that it? Well. You just let me tell you something, Young man. You will NEVER do better than my daughter, even if you had your pick of all the painted ladies up in the castle!"

She put her hands on her hips and glared at him. "And THAT'S if you were going to amount to anything in life! Imagine! A no account, poor excuse for a broke hunter..." Conner put his arm gently on his wife's shoulder. "Mamai.. there's something you should know.."

She twisted her shoulder sharply, shaking off his arm. "Oh, I know all right! Know when I see a no account, useless little BOY breaking my daughter's heart!" Lucinda rolled her eyes. "Mother, Stop! Regan isn't leaving because he doesn't want to be with me, He's leaving because he's the PRINCE!" Mamai glared at her daughter. "Don't you go defending that boy! He's nothing but a.. Prince?"

She stopped, looking confused. Regan stepped closer to her and nodded. "It's true, Mamai. I would give anything to not have to leave, but I cannot marry Lucinda." He smiled sadly. "I dearly wish I could be the man you had wanted me to be. Nothing would make me happier than to stay here with all of you, but I must go. Soon I will have to assume my duties at the castle and I fear if I linger much longer the Royal Guards will have to come and drag me back there." Mamai's jaw opened and closed and she blinked rapidly, not quite understanding yet.

"You're.. You're the Prince?" He smiled and gave his best courtly bow. "Prince Regan Von Dracomarfóir, at your service, Milady." She blushed brightly at the treatment, never having been bowed to before. Suddenly her face turned bright red.

"Oh! All the things I said to you! Oh.. Prince, I am SO sorry! Can you forgive me?" He smiled and took her hand, shaking his head. "No, Mamai. I could forgive you if you had done something wrong, but you did not. You were merely defending Lucinda and you would have been remiss not to." He sighed sadly. "I only hope that you will continue to protect her so fiercely until she finds a husband who can treat her as she deserves to be treated."

He smiled at the older woman. "Oh, and please, call me Regan. You did so willingly enough when you slapped my hand as I went to taste your wonderful pie filling!" She shook her head in amazement, turning to look at her daughter and husband.

"You both knew this, didn't you?" She asked, accusingly. Guiltily they both nodded. Connor cleared his throat. "We, um, we knew you would never be able to keep the secret, Dearest, so we decided to leave that bit of information for later."

Mamai narrowed her eyes dangerously. "We'll talk about this later. BOTH of you."

Regan picked up the bag of food and glanced at the door. He hesitated, not wanting to leave and yet knowing it was time to go. Finally Connor rolled his eyes.

"Well, go on and kiss her goodbye and then go, Boy." Regan pulled Lucinda close to him and kissed her then. It was a long, drawn out goodbye kiss, full of passion and longing.

"I will never forget you, Dearest Lucinda." He whispered into her ear after the kiss.

"Nor I you, Regan." She looked up into his eyes and smiled. "Remember to keep me close to you just as I will be keeping you close to me." With that he turned and walked out the door, forcing himself to not look back as he walked.

Chapter 12

Prince Regan sat on a large rock looking out over the crystalline blue waters of the mountain lake. He occasionally picked up a small rock and threw it in the water, watching the ripples as they widened out and disappeared, blending with the other small ripples caused by the breeze.

He thought of many things as he sat there. He imagined ruling the kingdom, he replayed the stories and pictures drawn by Araseth, but mostly he thought about Lucinda. What she would be doing then, wondering if she was thinking about him. He was so lost in thought he never heard the dragon approach.

"You have the look of someone who has lost something very dear to them, Young Prince."

Regan jumped visibly at the deep, rumbling voice in his ear, dropping the rock he was about to throw. He turned to look at Araseth, perched on his own rock, slightly above him. "I was just thinking about the girl I told you about, Araseth. I told her I wasn't going back any more. I had to say goodbye to her."

The dragon raised an eyebrow curiously. "You decided she was not the girl you wanted to make your mate, then?" Regan frowned and shook his head. "Not at all. I would love to.. to make Lucinda my mate. You know as well as I do that it is a forbidden thing. She's not royalty."

Araseth nodded sagely. "Oh, of course, of course. Who is it exactly that forbids royalty marrying non royals then?" Regan sighed and snapped. "I don't feel like playing your games, dragon. Everyone knows that it is a law unto the land that royalty must not marry below their station."

Again Araseth nodded. "And who makes these laws? Forgive me, I am not wise in the politics of man."

Regan sighed once more, a long, drawn out, sigh of resolution. He turned his head and stared at the dragon, speaking very slowly, as if to a child. "The laws are written by the consulate, a group of men who work to create the laws which we all live by. When they write a potential law they take it before the King who then considers it. If the new law makes sense to him he agrees and it is then written into the law books. Once it is written it becomes the Voice of the King, only able to be removed by him or his rightful heir. My father would NEVER remove that law from the books. He has preached to me his entire life that I must find a girl who has the proper station in life."

Araseth couldn't QUITE keep his lips from turning up in a slight smile, just a hint of fang showing. "So.. Once your Father passes into the next realm who will be deciding these types of things then?"

Regan rolled his eyes, exasperated. Finally he exploded. "I will, you senile old Dragon! Once my father dies it will all pass on to me. I will be the one who has the sole responsibility of deciding which laws rule the land!" Suddenly he blinked. "By the Gods.. it will be me. I can change any of the laws I want to!"

Araseth nodded, looking deeply into the boy's eyes. "Yes, youngling. It will be you. You will have all the power to change things you want. A bit of advice from a senile old dragon, though. Think not about the things you CAN change, because they will be many. Think instead of the things you SHOULD change, because those are what will make you a great King. The difference between can and should is the difference between tyrant and ruler. I will let you ponder that for a bit. Your mate is not gone from your life forever, Regan, unless you allow her to be. If truly you love her, nothing in the world should keep you from her, for life is to short to pass on true love, even for a dragon."

With that last statement he flapped his wings and lifted off into the growing shadows of the evening.

Chapter 13

For the next few days Lucinda was not her normal self. Some wondered if she was sick, her eyes seemed unusually red and she rarely smiled, going about her chores with a certain indifferent distractedness. Others, the more regular customers, noticed that Regan was nowhere to be seen and assumed that she was upset over a break up.

Connor and Mamai noticed as well, taking over most of the duties of working around the inn for a few days while Lucinda grieved. She took to taking long walks alone at night, always straying inevitably to the crumbling ruins of the old castle. She would sit for hours, thinking about Regan and missing his easy smile, his caring looks and his sometimes oddly shy sense of humor.

After several weeks had gone by a stranger came to the inn, panting and out of breath from running. He slammed the door open loudly, the cool air of early fall blowing past him, chilling the room. He held up a portrait of Prince Regan and yelled loudly to the crowded room.

"Has anyone seen this man? This is Prince Regan, Crown Prince of the Realm. I have an urgent message for him. It is vital I find him at once!"

The people in the inn crowded around the drawing, many gasping in surprise as they recognized Regan.

"Why, That's Regan! Sure enough we've seen him here, not for a long time, though. You should talk to Lucinda, maybe she knows where he's gone off to."

Conner made his way into the room, summoned by the commotion. "What's this all about?" He asked, facing the man. "Sir, These good folks tell me that the girl that works here, Lucinda, may know where the Prince is. It is vital we get a message to him. His father has fallen quite ill and is dying. He must get back to the castle at once. The King may only have days left to live!"

Lucinda gasped from the kitchen, hearing the man's words. "Oh, no! I have to let Regan know! If these men are all over looking for him they may accidentally find Araseth!" She ran to her room and hurriedly packed a few things. She turned to leave and saw Mamai standing there, watching her. "I have to go, Mother." She said. "Regan needs to hear this from someone who really cares about him."

The old woman stood silently for a moment. "Go then." She said simply. "I don't know how you hope to find him, but if anyone can do it, you can. Just be sure to come back to us safely, Lucinda." The girl smiled and nodded, pausing to kiss her mother on the cheek before she ran down the stairs and snuck out the back door. In truth, she had no idea where she was going, she only knew the general direction that Regan had headed off in, and a few vague references to where the dragon lived.

She looked around, getting her bearings, then she shrugged and headed off into the woods.

Chapter 14

She had walked for hours, the cold wind making her cloak snap and billow behind her, leaves and branches tangling in her hair as she walked down the faint game trails calling out his name. No one had answered, though, and the hour was growing late.

In the fall the days were much shorter and Lucinda found herself alone, in the woods, as darkness threatened the land. She shivered, looking around for a place to set up camp for the night. She called out once more in desperation as the last light of the day faded. Suddenly she saw a slight flicker of light ahead of her on the path. She moved closer, looking at it curiously as it hovered in front of her.

Soon she could make out the small figure of a girl, no larger than a mouse, hovering on gossamer wings in the middle of the trail. She gasped in shock. "By the Gods!" She uttered. "Regan was telling the truth. They really DO exist!"

A million thoughts ran through her head at once. She was tempted to run, faced with the truth that the creatures from the stories of her childhood were indeed, real. She was elated that Regan had been telling her the truth of what he had seen. She had wanted to believe him with all her heart, but..

"A real Faerie." She said softly, shaking her head in wonder. She approached the figure slowly, giving her best curtsy "Um.. excuse me, Miss.. um.. Faerie? Can you help me find Prince Regan? I have some very important news I must give him."

The tiny girl flitted over to her, looking her up and down curiously. She circled her slowly, judging her. Finally she hovered directly in front of Lucinda's face, staring into her eyes for a moment. Eventually she nodded her head, apparently satisfied. She turned and began flying down the faint trail, leaving the girl to follow her. Lucinda looked around and shrugged, then began following the creature from the stories of her youth.

Regan sat on a rock, listening, as usual, to another of Araseth's stories. He watched the images floating above the Dragon's head but his thoughts drifted back to Lucinda.

Suddenly a faint light came tearing through the canyon entrance, one of the faerie circling above his head wildly, trying to get his attention. He looked up at her curiously. "What is it, Marimo?"

He saw the urgency written on her tiny face. Fearing the worst he grabbed his bow and headed toward the entrance, following the tiny girl. As he got closer he saw a shadow moving in the darkness. Araseth's voice continued droning on as he told his tale in the background. Regan's eyes narrowed dangerously.

"If Marimo is so concerned it must be some sort of danger." He thought to himself. He moved silently closer to the moving shadow, slowly drawing his bow, a razor sharp arrow ready to pierce any creature intending to harm his friend. Marimo flew down and began circling the creature frantically. It waved its hands at her threateningly.

Regan went to one knee in the darkness, took a deep breath and sighted his bow. "A goblin!" He thought to himself, remembering Araseth's visions of the dark ones, the small, shambling creatures whose skin billowed about them constantly, moving like shadows in the darkness.

"One must have somehow found a way to escape the mountain. It must have somehow sniffed Araseth out!" His fingers began slipping easily from the string. He concentrated on his target, the arrow nearly ready to fly, to bring the foul creature down when suddenly a gust of wind caught the cloak and the hood slipped down, revealing a head of beautiful golden hair.

"Lucinda!" Realization came in a flash and he nearly let fly the arrow he had nocked in the bow. He let the bow go slack, dropping it as he ran toward the girl.

"Lucinda! What.. How?" She looked over at him as he ran to her and met him half way, wrapping her arms around him tightly, sobbing into his shoulder.

"Regan! I thought I would never find you! Your father's men- There are dozens of them out looking for you."

Regan's heart sank as he looked into her eyes, fearing the worst. "Father. Is he... ?"

She shook her head negatively. "No, but he's very ill. You must go home at once. They said he may only have days left to live." He took a deep breath and nodded. "Then I will leave tonight." He held her hands as he looked at her lovingly. "Thank you, Lucinda. Thank you for being the one to bring me the news. It is far less painful to hear from someone who I care so much about."

She wrapped her arms around him again, tightly. "I wish I could see you longer, Regan, but your father needs you now. You must go, before it is to late. It's a far walk to the castle from here."

There was a low, grumbling sound of a throat clearing from the shadows. "Not when you're on the back of a dragon." Araseth's soft voice rumbled from behind Regan.

He had moved closer in the darkness without anyone hearing. Lucinda jumped and let out a surprised squeak as she heard the voice and saw the sheer size of the dragon. "Is.. is this..?" She stammered in shock. Regan smiled at her reaction and nodded. "Araseth, I would like you to meet Lucinda, the girl you have been berating me for pining over all these weeks. Lucinda, this is Araseth, Lord of all dragonkind."

Araseth smiled briefly and dipped his head slightly toward the girl, his teeth shining brightly in the dim light. "It pleases me greatly to finally meet you, Lady Lucinda." He said, in his best courtly voice. "I only wish the circumstances were more pleasant."

His head swiveled to look at the Prince. "Now, Regan, gather your things and climb on my back. I will have you home before dawn." Regan shook his head stubbornly. "If you give me a ride the chances are good you will be seen, Araseth. I refuse to be the one responsible for you being discovered after all this time."

The dragon narrowed his eyes dangerously. "Prince Regan, I am quite old enough to make my own decisions, thank you. If it is Draco's will that I am seen and hunted down, so be it, but I will NOT sit here and watch my friend lose his last hours with his father because I am to afraid to do the right thing. Now, as sovereign King of all Dragonkind, I ORDER you to climb on my back so I can get you home!"

His voice rose in volume until it thundered through the small canyon, echoing off walls and dislodging small stones, which fell like a gentle rain on their heads. Lucinda squeaked softly and stepped back from the dragon, quaking in fear.

Regan rolled his eyes and moved over to her, wrapping his arm around her waist reassuringly. "Don't worry, Lucinda, he does this sort of thing a lot. He may hurt me if I don't listen to him, but he would never harm a hair on your beautiful head."

He smiled gratefully up at Araseth and bowed gracefully. "You win, My Lord. I will accept your kind offer with my thanks." Araseth Hmmphed and nodded. "You better show some respect, Youngling. A man hasn't ridden a dragon for over 500 years. Now, get on my back so we can take you home!"

Chapter 15

The childhood stories Regan was told as he lay in his bed at night were nothing compared to actual flight on the back of a dragon. In the stories it was always exciting, the wind rushing past your ears, the powerful muscles of the dragon beating steadily as you sat perched on his back riding into glorious battle.

Regan never expected it would be so blatantly terrifying. He sat, frozen in place as the great dragon lifted off the ground with him on his back. He tried to hide his fear, but Araseth must have noticed how tightly Regan was gripping his neck as he flew. His head swiveled back behind him and he looked at Prince Regan with an expression of amusement on his face as his wings flapped and the ground drifted further away.

"Oh, it isn't SO bad, is it, Prince? I promise, you are perfectly safe up here. There is nothing in the sky more mighty than a dragon."

Prince Regan chanced a quick look at the ground, setting his jaw tightly against the terror threatening to rise in the form of bile and leap out of his mouth. "I am not worried about up here, Dragon." He said tensely. "It is the rocks down below us that would smash me to jelly that concern me."

He heard the soft sound of the dragon chuckling faintly over the sound of wind whipping past his ears. He said nothing else the rest of the trip, merely held onto the great beast for all his life was worth until they landed in a small clearing in the woods just past the castle.

Regan climbed shakily off the back of the dragon, his stiff walk and ashen face telling all Araseth needed to know about how the Prince felt about flying. "Here you are, Youngling. You are a mere half a league from your home, in a fraction of the time. Say what you will about flying, but it is much quicker than travelling with those puny little twigs you humans call legs." He smiled down at Prince Regan. "Now, go. Attend to your father. Be a good son before you must be a good king. Remember all the things we've spoken of, Prince, and you will be a King of legend."

Regan looked up at the dragon for a moment, his face finally thawing enough for him to smile. "Araseth, I can not begin to tell you what these last few weeks have meant to me. You have taught me things I never dreamed any human would ever know again. You have been a good teacher and a good friend, and I will miss you greatly."

Regan swore he saw a slight blush under the rows of fine scales on the dragon's cheeks as he looked off into the distance for a moment.

"Regan, if my younglings had grown to adulthood I always hoped they would have the same strength of character you have shown me. Now, don't disappoint me, do you understand?"

And with that he was gone, the drafts from his wings chilling Regan as the great beast disappeared into the shadows of the night. He watched the sky for a moment after Araseth had gone, then he sighed and turned, picking out a faint trail leading toward the castle.

As he approached the lowered drawbridge he waved his hand in salute to the guard on duty. He heard the cry passing through the castle before he set his first step on the thick grey planks. He was quickly met with a rippling wave of humanity, all of the court advisors circled around him as soon as he entered the outer walls of the castle, all trying to give him advice and ask his opinions on things at one time.

Finally the Captain of the Guard shouted above the buzzing voices, scaring the assembled crowd to silence. "Enough!" He shouted. "The Kingdom can wait for a moment while the Prince regains his breath and sees his father." He looked at Regan seriously.

"King Domnhal has been asking for you, Prince. I fear his time is short. You should go sit by his side while he still knows you have made it back for him." Regan saw the expression on the Guard's face and nodded, excusing himself curtly and bounding up the stairs to his father's bed-chambers.

Chapter 16

Regan winced slightly as he walked into the King's rooms and caught the scent of illness as the slight breeze from the opened door stirred the stale air.

His father lay on the feather mattress, a once proud, strong man and now a frail shell, his face gray and thin as he lay upon his silken sheets. He looked as though he had passed from the world of the living already, his chest barely rising as he slept.

Prince Regan walked over and sat in the chair that had been placed beside the King's bed, reaching over and taking the King's wasted, frail hand in his own gently. What a difference being gone for one mere season had made on this once great ruler. The Prince studied his face as he slept, remembering the times he had spent with his father growing up. They were rare times, indeed, the raising of a son cut far to deeply into a ruler's time for much time spent, but the times that they had together had been ones that Regan would never forget.

His father had insisted on taking a rare few days from his duties and taking Regan for his first overnight trip to the woods, just the two of them. Domnhal had taught him how to fish then, and how to hunt. He smiled faintly as he remembered how proud he had been when he made his first kill, an old, sick rabbit that was to slow to get out of the way of a little boy's arrow. Most people would have thrown the poor thing out, there was little more left of it than skin and bones, and the meat was as tough as sun baked leather, but his father had treated that rabbit as if it was the finest fare ever brought to his table. They cleaned it together, his father and he, carefully preparing the rabbit for dinner. They cooked it over an open fire and shared his bounty, although, looking back, he shook his head ruefully, remembering how tough and tasteless it was.

At that time, though, it was the finest dinner in all the lands and he ate it proudly, chewing the leathery meat while his father praised him for the great hunter he was, the entire time straining to swallow the tough meat from the poor slain beast.

Domnhal opened his eyes slowly, feeling his son's strong hand wrapping his own cold one. He looked over into Regan's face and smiled weakly.

"I knew you would come, Son. Everyone has been telling me that you might not make it back in time, but I knew you would be here. Tell me about your adventures, Boy. Did you find yourself in your travels?"

Vindelar, the head of the brewer's guild was walking up to the King's chamber to check on his progress. He had been one of those that had given Regan such an evil glare on the night of the summer festival. He had not cared for the boy since he had been informed of Regan's comment at the judging about giving that peasant innkeeper the contract for making the royal mead.

He had sincerely hoped the prince had fallen awry of something in the forest, something hopefully fatal. To stack odds in his favor he had been speaking to Regan's cousin, Brenhold, knowing he was next in line for the throne if the Prince had met an untimely end. He had been in a meeting with the other brewers and had not heard of the Prince's return. He heard the King speaking with someone and paused, just outside the door, listening.

Regan stared down at his father for a moment, realizing he understood now the things that had driven the man relentlessly his entire life. He nodded slowly.

"I did, Father. I've had adventures that I find difficult to believe myself, and made a great many friends." He looked off out the window longingly.

"I met a girl." He said softly. "She's not of Royal blood, but she is an amazing lass. I was hoping I could bring her to the castle one day so the two of you could meet. I know you would adore her as much as I do."

Domnhal turned his head with great difficulty, his weakness showing even in such a small act. "You know the laws prevent you being with her, Son." He said softly. "Laws that my father's father approved and had written into the books. As your King I must tell you that you must forget her and find a girl with proper blood to carry on the royal lines."

He stopped speaking for a moment; a coughing fit taking his breath from him. Regan filled a glass with water and held it to his father's lips, the cough tapering off for a moment.

Regan nodded to his father, acknowledging the old man's words even as he felt his heart fall in his chest. "I know, Father. It is a forbidden union. I would not bring shame to your name by considering such a thing. She understands that as well."

The old man raised a finger, pausing Regan as he spoke. "Ah, you didn't let me finish, boy. I was going to say, as I lay here about to pass from this realm and see your mother again, I understand what folly that law is. Love is not something that you can set to paper and file in a legal system. Nor is it something that is reserved for only those with the proper bloodlines. Love is something that is experienced far to little in this life, Boy. If this girl means so much to you and you KNOW in your heart it is the right thing to do, then change the law. That's what I've been trying to teach you all these years, Regan. People will look to you to lead them through the good times as well as the bad times.

In your heart you know the right and wrong things to do. Don't let some stuffy old moldering books tell you right from wrong, you already know. In here."

The old man reached out with a trembling hand and tapped Regan on his chest. "Be a leader, boy. You can change many things in your life, but think carefully before you do. Decide first if those things should be changed for the good of the people, or for your own benefit."

Regan recoiled a bit at those words, so similar to the ones he had heard from Araseth.

"Father! That's the other thing I have to tell you about. I saw.. I met a dragon! He allowed me to ride on his back to get back to you. Did you know dragons can SPEAK, Father? We conversed for hours. In many ways he reminded me of you."

The King's eyes widened in fright as Regan spoke, looking around to make sure no one had entered the room. He waved Regan to silence desperately.

"Regan! Do not speak of such things! You know my time is short and once I pass you must sit the Throne for 2 full seasons as a trial of your right to lead the people. If someone overheard you talking about dragons you could easily find yourself removed on the basis of insanity and your cousin ascending in your place. "

He narrowed his eyes dangerously. "And if that were to happen it is customary that the Sovereign who has been proven unfit to lead is executed so the bloodlines of the royal family stay true. Please.. Son.. There are already those who do not care for you and detest the thought of you as their King. Do not give them any reason to call your sanity into question!"

Vindelar stood outside the door of the Royal chambers, a slow, wicked smile curling over his lips as he overheard the softly spoken conversation. He turned on his heel and walked away quickly. With any luck he would be able to find Brenhold. He had a feeling that this evening's dinner was going to hold some very interesting conversations.

Regan nodded, standing and closing the door after checking outside to make sure no one was around. He went back and sat down again, smiling reassuringly down at his father.

"No need to worry now, Poppa. There is no one around to hear us. Its just you and I." He proceeded to tell his father about his adventures, describing in detail all the stories the mighty dragon had related. When he was finished Domhal looked up at him with a serious expression.

"Regan- Son, it is truly an incredible tale you have told me, and one which, if true, demands that as an honorable man you find a way to help that dragon. The fact that a creature who used to be an ally of humanity has suffered such an injustice is unforgivable, but the fact that he suffered it at the hands of one of our ancestors is something that cannot be forgotten. You must find a way to correct this injustice and cleanse the blood from our family's hands in the eyes of the ones on the Other Side.."

Regan looked down at his father and nodded. "You have my word, Father. I know not how, but I will not fail you. You have my word." He smiled down at his father tenderly, knowing the man was not much longer for this world.

"Now, why don't we talk about more pleasant things? It has been far too long since we sat and chatted." They talked long into the night then, as only a father and his son can, laughing and crying together for the last time until Domnhal's eyes couldn't stay open any longer. Regan smiled at his father one last time as the old man drifted off to sleep.

He leaned down and placed a gentle kiss on his cheek. "Sleep well, Father. Mother is waiting to see you with open arms on the other side." He stood then and walked to his rooms in silence, wearily undressing and laying down in his bed.

Chapter 17

King Domhal died that night. He went quietly, in his sleep, greeted warmly by his Queen and accompanied in his final walk to the other side by all of those he had known and loved in his life that had gone before him.

Prince Regan was informed at first light. He accepted the news stoically, thanking the servant that brought him the news.

He sat for a moment in silence, thanking his father for all the wisdom he had imparted to him during his life. Finally he stood and splashed some cold water on his face from the basin. He dressed himself and sighed deeply, mustering the courage to face his destiny. Finally he opened the door and stepped out to face the crowd of sympathetic subjects.

He nodded and graciously thanked them for the offered condolences and then finally moved to speak to the chamberlain about funerary arrangements. The death of a King was not a simple occasion. Preparations had begun the moment it was announced that King Domhal hadn't long to live. Runners were sent out to the far corners of the Kingdom and throngs of subjects, both royal and common, had been streaming into the courtyard in a steady procession for the last day.

After the arrangements had been discussed, Connagal, the Chamberlain, waved everyone out of the room and closed the door. He looked at Regan and bowed deeply. He spoke in a somber, ceremonial voice. "Sire, the time has come for me to present you with the crown of the Realm. You will wear this for the span of 2 seasons in the trust of the People that you are found fit and able to perform your duties to the Kingdom. During this time, if sufficient proof of your inability to lead the people arises, the closest member of the royal family has the authority to question you in your position and a trial will be held to determine who has been given the providence to lead our people.

It has been this way for countless generations and, Gods willing, will be this way for many more. Do you accept the responsibilities of the position of King of this realm?"

Regan looked at his old friend and paused for a moment. The thought of leaving, running away to go live with Lucinda and be a hunter for the rest of his life while Brenhold got stuck dealing with the Kingdom was most tempting, but eventually his sense of duty won out. "I do." He said simply.

Connagal nodded solemnly and raised the crown, setting it on Regan's head. "Then with the power vested in me as Chamberlain of the Royal House of Midrealm I pronounce you King Temporum until such a time as your status will be made permanent."

Regan nodded in acceptance and smiled at his friend. "Shall we have a mead together before the throngs come back, Connagal? It has been far too long since we've had a chance to talk. Come, let's raise a glass in Father's honor."

The chamberlain cleared his throat awkwardly, looking uncomfortable. "Um.. That is not permitted any more, Sire. The King takes no food or drink with any company besides other Royals." Regan rolled his eyes and looked at the older man.

"Connagal, you gave me my first glass of mead! And what is this 'Sire' nonsense. You're my oldest friend. Please call me by my proper name, at least when we are alone together."

Again the man shook his head negatively. "I must not, Sire." He looked at Regan pleadingly. "We've discussed this in the past, don't you remember? I am but a servant to the King. Before you were crowned it was allowed for the two of us to associate with each other. It was part of my duties to help you grow into a man fit to sit upon the throne. Now, though, you are the sovereign of the land and if it were overheard I was being to familiar with you I could be called before a tribunal according to our realm's law and punished for it."

He looked around carefully; making sure no one was listening at the door. "Regan, " He said softly, "I ask you this one last thing as a friend. We cannot be familiar with each other anymore or it could mean my life. I've watched you grow up and I am very proud of you. I have no doubt you will be an inspiring leader to our people, but we cannot be familiar with each other any more. I would ask you, as a friend, to please.. please treat me as your servant. From now on you will be addressed by your formal title at all times, Sire. It is simply the way things are."

Regan looked at his friend for a moment and then sighed, nodding. "Very well, Chamberlin." He emphasized the word slightly out of sarcasm, "If that is the way it must be, then that is the way it is. Please, fetch me a glass of mead so I may toast my good fortune at having gained this accursed crown at the expense of keeping my oldest friend."

Chapter 18

Regan stood outside the door to the Pathway, scowling slightly as he waited to be announced.

Shortly after he had dismissed Connagal a swarm of dressing staff had come into his chambers to prepare him for the official presentation to the public. He was washed carefully, shaved, perfumed, and dressed in layers of brightly colored velvet robes as the crown was carefully placed on his head. He then had the Sword of his office strapped around his waist.

He drew the pathetic little blade and shook his head at the feel of it. Obviously it had never been designed for actual use, the weight and balance of it were atrocious, all the gold and gems decorating the handle throwing the entire blade off of any sort of balance whatsoever. He dropped it back into the jeweled scabbard disdainfully, rolling his eyes in disgust.

"I'm certainly glad I have royal bodyguards around me." He thought. "If I ever had to try to use that ridiculous thing I would be run through before I ever managed to get it into guard position."

Just then he heard the voice of the Chamberlain, announcing his arrival. The massive twin gold filigreed doors swung open and he looked over the crowd assembled in the presentation room. He walked regally down the aisle, looking forward, head held high as he felt every eye in the room looking upon him. He ascended the steps and turned to face the masses for a moment before speaking in a loud, clear voice.

"Last night my father passed from this realm. He was a good King. He spent every moment of his life trying to make this Kingdom the best in all the Realms. For the good of everyone I intend to continue his quest. I shall not shirk my duties, nor shall I abandon my people for any reason. Fate has decreed that I am your King and so shall I be, until I am no longer fit to fulfill my duties to my people."

He looked over the crowd for a moment, meeting their eyes with his own. He saw doubt written on some faces, hope on others, open scorn on a few of them. He smiled slightly as he noticed the traditional pattern of the court, minor nobles and business owners in front, farmers, hunters and tradesmen in the back. He cleared his throat, a sudden, reckless feeling coming over him.

"As my first official duty as King I would ask that in the future court be assembled in the following way; From now on the business of commoners will be taken care of first, so their time away from their trades and fields be limited as much as possible when it is necessary for them to come to court. Business owners with multiple workers will be heard second, as their trade can continue without them for a bit longer without burdening them. Nobility will be heard from last from now on."

He felt a guilty pang of pleasure as a collective gasp went through the crowd, a mix of shock, surprise and outrage could be seem openly on the faces of the people toward the front. He sat then, sinking deeply into the cushioned chair that, in his mind, still belonged to his father. He failed to notice the look of cold hatred that Vindelar was giving him.

Chapter 19

Later, after the official presentation Regan was seated behind closed doors with his panel of advisors. He sat, arms crossed over his chest as he listened to them rant.

"Sire! You cannot DO things like that!" Reinhold, an old, balding mage with a long white beard protested. "A new King does not make changes on the day of his coronation. It is simply not done! Remember, you are still sitting Temporum for 2 full cycles. You must not give those who would unseat you any cause to do so."

The rest of the advisors nodded in agreement. Regan shrugged, looking over at the old man.

"Well, it is done now, Reinhold. If I were to reverse my decision even if I thought it were the right thing to do, it would show weakness and indecision in front of my subjects. Besides, I still feel it was the right thing to do and therefore I stick by my words."

A red faced, hefty man pounded on the table for attention. "Sire, we all respect that you were trying to make a choice for the betterment of the people, but by doing so you have offended the entirety of the nobility of the realm. With all due respect, Sire, while I appreciate your concern for the commoners, they do not have the power to unseat your rule. The nobles do. Do not forget, many of the wealthier merchants are also nobility and therefore they, too, will have to wait in the back of the chambers until last to address you. These are very powerful people, My Liege. It will not be good to have them as enemies. In fact, I have already heard rumblings of dissatisfaction about your leadership. If there is any reason at all for them to oppose your rule I assure you, they will not hesitate to take advantage of it and put Brenhold on the throne in your stead."

King Regan shrugged. "Then so be it. I will not rule with fear in my heart, controlled by small men with big ideas. If they are to attack me, I say let them come and we will settle our differences like men!"

The advisors all looked at each other and shrugged in resignation. "If that is your wish, My Liege, so it shall be. I only hope you can stand under the buffering of what can be a very vile group of players."

Suddenly there was a knock on the door. All present looked at each other in surprise. It was highly unusual for someone to violate the sanctity of the inner meeting chambers.

Finally Regan stood and walked to the door, barely getting it cracked wide enough for a man to pass before Vindelar strode in, his face a mask of rage. He held up a clay bottle with a broad gesture. It bore the mark of the Day's Ride inn.

"What is the meaning of this?" He demanded angrily. "I found an entire case in the kitchens when I was conducting my annual inspection! Which of you has violated the rules and brought this peasant slop into our pantries? This is a clear violation of the agreement the Royal house has made with the Brewer's guild and I won't stand for it!"

Regan shut the door quietly and turned to face Vindelar. "The mead is mine, Vindelar." He said quietly. "I sent one of my personal guard out to fetch it for me. I have grown quite fond of it since I dined there frequently while I was away. It is for no one else but me, it poses no threat to you or your precious agreements."

Vindelar looked up at King Regan, his dislike for the man barely concealed. He took a deep breath to compose himself and nodded quickly. "I understand your fondness for this local.. brew, My Liege, but under the contracts written by your grandfather, King Tiberius, no brewed beverages shall be placed into the castle's inventory until it has been inspected by the guild master. This order was put in place to protect our beloved Royal family from any accidental poisoning or sickness due to incorrectly brewed wine, mead or ale. I'm sure the King was merely ignorant of this rule. I will have the offending bottles removed at once, until a proper inspection can be performed. At that time we will interview the maker of this mead, inspect his facilities, and offer him guild membership. Once he pays the 500 florin charge to join the guild his product will once again be allowed into the royal kitchens.

In the meantime might I send you a case of my finest mead, personally crafted by me, the Master Brewer of the Realm? I assure you, it will be much more pleasing to your palette than this gutter swill."

Regan raised an eyebrow as he looked down at Vindelar. "So what you are saying, Vindelar, unless I am mistaken, is that you intend to confiscate the mead that I ordered brought here, and then, if I want his brew back you will bury him in bureaucracy, break him with 'guild charges', fail his inspections and drive him out of business unless he falls into line with exactly what you want, in which case I may have his mead returned to me in.. how long?"

Vindelar shifted uncomfortably, averting his eyes from the King's gaze. "Oh, the process is reasonably quick, My King. The whole thing should not take more than 6 or 7 cycles, as long as the brewer complies with our rules."

Regan nodded slowly, thinking. Finally he spoke again. "Well, Vindelar, How about this instead? I understand those rules are in place for a reason and I am quite willing to work within the system, but I AM quite fond of that mead and I know the brewer rather well. Why don't you leave the case I purchased right where it is, call it an oversight if you will, take the bottle that you have in your hand to conduct your quality inspection, expedite your inspection of his facilities, and I personally will pay the guild fee for his entrance. If we go about it that way I should think the whole thing can be done in, oh, say, 2 weeks? That should coincide perfectly with me running out of this rogue case in my kitchen.

In the meantime, please, feel free to send that case of your best. It might be amusing to have a little friendly competition. I'm curious to see if my untrained palate can tell 'gutter swill' from the finest mead in the realm."

Regan put his hand on Vindelar's shoulder, opening the door. The smaller man looked around in confusion, not entirely sure what just happened. Regan guided him through the door, closing it lightly behind him.

"Thank you again for bringing this matter to our attention, Master Brewer. I have every confidence you will resolve this situation with the utmost urgency." The door clicked shut softly and Vindelar glared daggers at the rough wood. "That does it, My good King." He sneered, muttering softly. "I think it is high time you found out what happens when you don't play by the right set of rules. We won't have to worry about getting your precious little meadery accepted into the guild, because you are going to be off the throne in a matter of hours." He turned and strode purposefully away, searching out Brenhold to begin his plan.

King Regan turned from the closed door and returned to his seat, his advisors looking at him in a mix of admiration and doubt.

"Now, good advisors, where were we before we were interrupted?" He asked, looking around the table. Reinhold sighed. "My Liege, after observing that little conference you just had with Vindelar it becomes obvious that you did, in fact, learn something from your father. However, I feel I must warn you; he did not like the outcome of your conversation. I fear you have just made a powerful enemy over something so small as a glass of mead."

Regan chuckled. "Reinhold, My friend, have you ever tasted Vindelar's mead? The stuff is awful! THAT is no small matter. Besides, these rules that have been put in place over all these past cycles have become stifling for the common folk of the Kingdom, benefitting only those who have the necessary means to work within the established system.

While I'm sure they were formed with the best possible intentions, these rules have been twisted over the centuries by greedy men so they only benefit a few. While that conversation may have been about mead, gentlemen, the larger discussion is actually about the future of our Kingdom. In my views we all wear the same skin, King and commoner alike, so let us begin weeding out the things that make some men rich while others struggle to feed their families, shall we?

Now, let me send down to the kitchens for a bottle of Day's Ride mead, and let us toast to letting honest men do honest work."

Chapter 20

The coronation festival was held that evening. It was a traditional formal affair, which occurred whenever a new King was installed into his position.

It was one of the only times that common folk were allowed to mix with Royalty, all citizens of the Kingdom who were able to attend brought small gifts to present to their new sovereign.

King Regan sat on a small raised platform, his face muscles cramping from his constant smile of gratitude, thanking all the well wishers for their gifts whether they were as small as a dozen eggs or as extravagant as the beautifully engraved dragon bone handled sword he was presented by the head of the artists' guild.

He was engaged in a particularly boring conversation about the future of trade relations with Secondshire when he heard a voice that caused his heart to leap into his mouth. "An offering, My King." Lucinda said softly, laying a bundle of freshly picked aromatic wild flowers and herbs on the floor next to him.

His smile was genuine as he politely excused himself from the conversation and turned to her. "Lucinda! Its good to see you! I've missed you!"

She blushed and looked around, noting the glares she was being given by the maidens of the court who had been trying to capture his attention all evening. "King Regan, " She said, emphasizing the word King a bit. "I hope you find my offering pleasing to you. Thank you, My Lord, for noticing."

Regan almost admonished her for her formality, wanting nothing more than to hold her in his arms once again, and then he remembered where they were and noticed the looks she was getting from members of the court. He took a breath, composing himself before he nodded to her, still not quite able to keep the smile from his face.

"I find your gift most pleasing, Lucinda, and I thank you for attending this festival. Be sure to offer your parents my greetings and hopes that they will prosper during my coming reign."

She nodded, leaning close and whispering to him before walking away. "Look inside the bundle. There is something in there I didn't think you would want to share with everyone." Then she smiled and winked at him, just a hint of the reckless, sarcastic expression she had given him on the first night they met and she walked away, blending into the crowd.

Curiously he reached down, acting like he was inspecting the gift of flowers and herbs. Tucked inside was a small golden heart necklace. He smiled and slipped it dexterously into his sleeve. Soon he was once again engaged in conversations ranging from how high he thought the new cycle's tariffs were going to be to how the peach coloring of a particularly insistent maiden's gown truly did bring out the blue in her eyes. He glanced around the room occasionally, sometimes catching the briefest glimpse of Lucinda as she moved around the room.

After a bit he heard Brenhold's arrival being announced and he sighed in relief. Brenhold always seemed to do a better job of drawing the merchants' attention than he did. He might possibly have a moment to relax. That pleasant thought left his head immediately though, when he saw the expression on his cousin's face and noticed he was walking in the company of Vindelar.

Brenhold approached him and looked at him oddly. "A moment of your time, Sire?" He asked, stiffly. "In private, if you don't mind." Regan was confused at his cousin's attitude and tone, but nodded. "Of course, Cousin. Right this way."

The two of them moved over into a private council chamber, shutting the door behind them. Regan never noticed the guards taking up their positions at either side of the door.

As soon as the door clicked shut King Regan looked at his cousin curiously. "What's this about, Brenhold?" The other man looked around to make sure they were alone in the room. He took a breath and began speaking.

"Vindelar has made some accusations, Regan. Serious accusations. He's sworn an oath in front of witnesses that your sanity is in question."

Regan looked at Brenhold in shock. "What? My sanity?" He started laughing. "This is over a dispute about mead, Brenhold! The man is truly off his nut! We had a discussion earlier about trade practices of the brewer's guild. That is all. Its nothing."

Brenhold got a pained expression on his face. "It's not nothing Cousin." He said urgently. "He has sworn in front of witnesses he overheard you speaking to your father on his deathbed, talking about wild, crazy things. He said you claimed you had met a dragon.. and not only that, the dragon could speak and you had talked with him for days. If this is true it brings an honest question about your sanity, Regan. Please.. between you and I, tell me you were wandering through the woods drunk. Tell me you are completely aware it was a drunken blur of a night and you were talking to a bat you thought was a dragon and Vindelar misheard you."

Regan's mouth dropped open in shock. "He.. I.. I was talking with Father. There was nothing said that was meant for any other ears, Brenhold."

His cousin nodded his head in understanding. "I understand completely, Regan. You were telling your father a funny story on his deathbed so he could chuckle as he made his way into the afterlife."

Regan paused for a moment. All he had to do was agree with his cousin and the matter would be swept under a rug, Vindelar's testament ignored completely. None would dare question the words of two members of the Royal family on such a matter. He actually considered it, briefly. Finally he sighed and shook his head. Araseth had suffered enough in his life. Regan could not bear the thought of telling further falsehoods regarding him, even if the results were unfavorable to him. Besides, he had given his father his solemn oath that the ancient wrongs his family had done would be corrected.

He set his jaw resolutely and shook his head. "No, Brenhold, he speaks the truth. It was a secret meant to stay between my father and I, but he heard truly. I have met a dragon. His name is Araseth and he is the King of their race. He and I did speak for long periods of time. He is quite wise, actually, and a creature I am proud to call a friend."

Brenhold looked at the floor and shook his head despondently, sighing deeply. "And you will not change your story, Regan?"

King Regan shook his head negatively. "I don't suppose you would be willing to lead a hunting party out to prove the truth of your tale, either?" He looked up, into Regan's eyes hopefully.

Regan met his look coolly. "I would rather die first, Brenhold." He said calmly. "I will not destroy such a fine creature to prove I was telling the truth of things."

Brenhold took a deep breath, looking away. "Then you know I will have to acknowledge Vindelar's accusations publicly. You will be tried by a tribunal of nobles and if found unable to function in your position as King, as the law dictates clearly, you will be executed publicly so no one may question the decision in the future and blur the lines of our leadership."

Regan reached out and placed his hand on his cousin's shoulder. "I understand, Brenhold, and I don't blame you. Know this, though. Someone besides me needs to understand if I am executed. Dragons still live, my friend, and they mean us no harm. Araseth went into hiding because he wanted no further troubles between his race and ours.

We slaughtered his entire family.. No, his entire race because of a misunderstanding, Brenhold. Promise me this, as your cousin. You've always known when I was lying to you, even when we were children. Know the truth now. He exists and merely wants to be left to himself. I would have your word he will be left in peace, no matter what happens to me."

Brenhold stared deeply into his cousin's eyes, finally nodding. "I think you are convinced of the truth of your tale, Cousin, and I will make you the vow there will be no hunting parties sent out to verify the truth of your tale. As your cousin and friend I can tell you, though, I highly advise you lie during the tribunal. Say you were drunk. Its no secret I've always thought I would make a better King than you, Regan, but I never wanted that position this way."

Regan smiled and hugged his cousin tightly. "Thank you, Bren. If it is my time to travel to the afterworld I will do so with a song in my heart, knowing I can trust my cousin and friend."

Brenhold smiled sadly, nodding. "Yes, you can trust me, Cousin. Now, we better go before the guards outside break the door down and make a scene dragging you to the Judgement." Regan nodded and, head held high, glanced into his cousin's eyes once more and opened the door, walking out to face his fate proudly.

The guards had taken him by each arm as he walked from the room, leading him quietly to the raised stage originally set up for the banquet to follow his introduction.

The Chamberlain was carefully handed a scroll by Brenhold. He unrolled it curiously, nearly dropping the parchment as his mouth fell open in shock while his eyes scanned the page. He looked at Brenhold questioningly. Brenhold nodded somberly. "Just read it, Connagal."

He said softly. The Chamberlain nodded, his voice cracking a bit as he began to read. He stopped and then started once more. "Hail, good people of Midrealm! Put down your drinks and offer me your ears. This once festive occasion has come to a somber end, for we now have serious business to discuss. Vindelar, Master Brewer, Duke of Elliot, High brewer of the Kings libations, brings an accusation to be heard by an official tribunal. He accuses King Temporum Regan Von Dracomarfóir of Lunacy and demands he be removed from the throne at once so he causes no further harm to the Kingdom. His accusations have been heard by Lord Brenhold Dracomarfoir who has agreed to stand as King should the tribunal decide the charges are justified. If this is the case King Temporum Regan Von Dracomarfoir will be hanged in a public execution without benefit of a hood so all may witness his demise and never question the decision of the Tribunal. The Judgement will begin at high sun tomorrow. As of this moment the Presentation is over. Please return to your homes."

A collective gasp went through the crowd as they watched Regan's hands being bound in chains. He continued holding his head high as he was led through the crowd toward the dungeons. As he looked over he saw Lucinda, her mouth open in shock, a tear running down her cheek. He offered her a small, sad smile as he was led from the room.

Chapter 21

The dungeon was cold and damp and Regan shivered even though the guards had provided him with a cot and extra blanket. He sat on the edge of the small cot, staring out the tiny window high up on the wall. He watched the stars pass slowly in front of the tiny slit for quite some time. Finally the moon crept past the edge of the sill, allowing a thin sliver of light into the room. Regan remembered the tiny gold heart Lucinda had given him and he pulled it out of his sleeve, smiling as it gleamed in the darkness.

He sighed sadly as he stared at the tiny necklace. "I should have stayed out there with you, Fairest one." He said softly. "We should have run away together. I only wanted to make the Kingdom a better place for all to live in and now I'm afraid I have lost you forever. My last hope is for you to be close to the gallows as I die, so I may look into your eyes once again as I pass from this world." He closed the tiny heart in his hand, holding it close to himself as he lay back on the hard cot and watched the moonlight flow slowly across the wall, passing the time. Finally he drifted into a restless sleep, never letting go of the heart she had given him.

They came early for him the next day. The guards appeared as the first light of dawn appeared on the horizon, sounding almost apologetic for retrieving him at such an early hour. "The Panel has assembled, your Highness." One of them said simply. "Its time to go." Regan sat up his eyes still bleary from lack of sleep. He simply nodded and stood, following the guards. He was led to a small room with a wash-basin and a change of clothing and he cleaned and dressed himself quickly.

A member of the kitchen staff appeared, asking him nervously if she could get him something to eat before he faced the Panel. He smiled at her and shook his head. "My apologies, Anna, but the mere thought of food lies heavy on my belly at the moment. Nothing for me now, Thank you."

She nodded and scurried of nervously. Regan knew it was a violation for any of the staff to speak to him before a Judgement and so he was touched by the gesture, even if he had no intention of accepting it. He met the guards once more outside the door and they escorted him into the Judgement chamber. It was a cold stone room with a single seat in front and elevated tiers of seating around the room.

The panel of 12 was already seated, waiting for him. Off to the left Vindelar sat, a smug smile on his face as he watched Regan enter. As he walked into the room his eyes met each of the members of the panel, judging them by their expression. The friendliest look he saw was doubt, followed by scorn, anger and a trace of fear.

He looked deliberately at Vindelar and nodded curtly before walking to the front of the room and taking his seat. Brenhold stood, in charge of the proceedings due to his new status as King Temporum until the Judgement was delivered.

Brenhold cleared his throat and began speaking: "My fellow members of the court, we come here today to listen and determine whether the accusations of Lord Vindelar Mimestoff, Master brewer and head of the Brewer's guild, are significant enough for a Judgement against Regan Von Dracomarfóir, Former King Temporum of Midrealm, to be removed from his position as our leader. Furthermore, as dictates of law clearly state, if his accusations are judged to be with merit Regan Von Dracomarfóir will be executed publicly as the sun drops below the horizon 5 days from this date. Are there any here who do not feel qualified to sit on this panel to pass Judgement?"

Brenhold looked around the room, meeting the eyes of everyone present. He knew very well none would back out of the proceedings, this would guarantee the status of all present once the Judgement was passed. More than likely there had been several pounds of coins passed around just to be able to secure a spot in this hall by many of them. After a few moments of silence he nodded.

"Very well then, since you all know the ramifications of a hasty decision, let us proceed. We will hear first from Vindelar." He looked at the pointy little man directly. "You may begin telling your story, Sir."

Vindelar cleared his throat and nodded, standing nervously. "Well, Sire, I was making my way up to the King's chambers. I knew he had been very sick lately so I stopped by every day to wish him good health. I was just about to knock on the door when I heard Pri.. I mean.. Regan's voice coming from inside the room. Since I didn't want to disturb them since the Pri.. Regan had been gone for so long I waited until they were done speaking before I entered the room. "

Regan glared at the little brewer, muttering under his breath. "Stood outside spying, you mean." Brenhold turned and gave Regan a cool look. "You will have your chance to speak, Regan. Until then I suggest you be silent and listen or you will be removed from this room until your accuser has had his chance to speak."

Regan threw his hands up into the air and stood, angrily. "To what point, Cousin?" He asked, glaring over at Vindelar. "So I can let my 'accuser' tell the panel exactly what I am going to agree with?" He turned to look at the panel of nobles. "I say let us save some time, shall we? Vindelar is going to tell all of you that he 'innocently' overheard me speaking to my father IN CONFIDENCE about the things I had seen while I was traveling.

Point in fact, he is going to tell all of you I made wild claims to not only seeing a dragon, but to speaking with him as well. Instead of listening to his boring second hand tale, why don't I just fill all of you in on what I've seen and then you can make your decision. Yes, I have met a dragon. His name is Araseth and he was the Lord of the dragons until my Great Grandfather made a mistake and saw fit to hunt them all down and kill them in cold blood.

He had a mate and children and he watched them all be slaughtered mercilessly in front of his eyes while he lay there wounded and unable to defend them."

Brenhold winced at the outburst, realizing there was no containing his cousin's lunacy anymore. A collective gasp of shock went through the room at the accused's outburst. All present expected a long series of accusations and denials.

They expected Regan to counter Vindelar's accusations, claim the man had overheard incorrectly, even plead and beg for mercy from the assembly. For most of them in the room the decision had been made before they ever sat down, purchased by the coins that had been delivered by Vindelar's servants the evening before. Instead, the former King continued speaking.

"In addition he told me of the Time before history, when dragons and men lived together in peace. How they fought together against the dark forces from another place that were trying to take this land for their own."

He strode over and looked down into the startled eyes of one of the petty noblemen he had been speaking to about trade relations just over 10 hours before. He smiled at him and shook his head. "But you don't believe me, do you, Renifer? You don't believe such a thing is possible. I mean, a dragon, after all? After all these years? How is that possible? Why hasn't he attacked the castle, sought vengeance if I'm telling a true story, am I correct?"

The noble's eyes widened in fright and he tried to speak, only nonsensical gibberish coming from his lips as he sat in shock at being singled out. Finally he shrugged, even as he shrank back a bit in his chair from the one he clearly considered mad.

Regan chuckled, shaking his head in disdain at the man. He stepped back and looked around the room once again. "I'll tell you why. It was because that dragon is ten times the man of any of us in this room. The dragons never wanted war with us. They only wanted to be left alone. The 'dragon attacks' from our history books were from two rogue dragons which had been judged and executed by the rest of the dragons before Great grandfather ever even heard about the attacks. Point in fact, it was we humans, not the dragons who were at fault, and who continue to be at fault by spreading false stories to children about how horrible they are."

Brenhold's eyes narrowed in anger at the accusation the folk heroes of their history were actually cold-blooded killers who were entirely in the wrong. "Be careful, cousin." He said coolly. "You tread on dangerous land, insulting our ancestors in such a way."

Regan laughed, looking over at his cousin. "Bren, Cousin, I'm afraid I have passed dangerous land long ago. You see, the outcome of this entire event has already been decided by those who sit in power and are afraid I may take some of it away from them and give it to those more deserving."

He looked over at Vindelar and smiled, noticing the ratty little man paling as he squirmed in his chair. "Isn't that right, Vindelar?" he asked, curiously. "I wonder how many pounds of gold passed through your fingers to some of these fine individuals in this room to assure they made the right decision."

The brewer shook his head sharply and squeaked. "Of.. of course not, Regan. I was only concerned about the good of the Kingdom.."

Regan smiled and nodded, saying sarcastically, "Of course you were, Good Sir! You would NEVER put your wealth above the Kingdom's best interests, would you? None of this has a thing to do with the fact if I am removed and my cousin is seated on the throne you will be able to continue gouging the entire kingdom for the swill you pass off as fine liquor with no ramifications or fair competition possible."

He turned once again to face the Judgement panel. "And as far as the rest of you milk sopped crumb lickers go, if this is TRULY a fair Judgement you will listen to what I'm about to tell you next." He looked around at all the shocked and angry expressions in the room, his eyes finally settling on the enraged face of his cousin.

"Mhirachor has reappeared." He said softly. "The castle of the dragons is once again in our world. All you need do is send a rider out to confirm it exists and all of my stories will be proven true."

Brenhold shook his head, sighing sadly. "Regan, sit down." He commanded. Regan walked proudly over and sat once again in the seat of Judgement. Brenhold stared at him for a moment before speaking.

"Well, Cousin, your testimony has now insulted the members of this panel, the members of the royal house, the entire merchant's guild, AND out Great Grandfather. Perhaps in closing you would like to say something bad about your mother?"

He turned to the Panel. "Having heard Regan's rather um .. boisterous testimony is the Panel prepared to debate a Judgement?" One of the older members of the Panel stood and nodded. "I believe we are ready to form a Judgement, Your Highness. If the accused and the accuser could be escorted from the room, Please?"

Brenhold nodded and motioned to the guards who walked over and stood next to Regan. He stood calmly, walking between them as he was escorted out the door. As he passed Renifer he paused, leaning down to whisper into the man's ear. "Oh, Renifer? Just as an added note I heard all these stories about our past while a particularly comely faerie was sitting on my knee. Her name is Marimo. I think you two would get along famously. She doesn't say much either." He winked and straightened, walking from the room proudly.

In the next room Regan stood, waiting on word Judgement had been passed. He was not nervous, as he expected to be. A kind of calm had settled over him after he had spoken. True, his words would likely mean his execution, but at least he had said what had needed to be said for 2 hundred years.

While he was waiting Vindelar was escorted into the room as well, kept well to the other side of the room by the guards. He stared at Regan incredulously, a grin appearing on his face. "You really ARE insane, Regan! I had only hoped to make you look so for the panel, but I needn't have bothered. You did this to yourself!"

Regan smiled across the room at Vindelar. "I merely said what has needed to be said for centuries, Vindelar. Perhaps I will die, but eventually the truth of things will come out and I will be vindicated. I will go to my rest knowing I have done the right thing in my life and therefore will pass through the gates. I truly wonder., where do you think you will end up, after this pathetic life of yours ends?"

Vindelar opened his mouth to retort, then closed it again, paling a bit. He cleared his throat and glared at Regan. "Its just as well. You would have ruined the Kingdom with your crazy ideas about making it a better place for everyone. If you only learn one lesson in this life, Regan, take THIS to your afterlife. There are those who are destined to have the entire world in their hands, and there are those who are fated to fill our hands with the world." He grinned wickedly. "I guess we'll never know which one you would have been, will we?"

Regan stared at the brewer coldly. "I will break you one day, Vindelar. You and your kind have seen your time in this world. It is time for the next cycle to begin. The Kingdom will see you for the sneaking cowardly vermin you truly are." Vindelar threw his head back and laughed. "You'll be dead in five days, you fool King. Unless I develop a sudden fear of ghosts I don't think I have a thing to worry about!"

Just then the door opened and a solemn Brenhold entered. "The panel has reached an agreement, Regan. They are ready to pass your Judgement now."

Vindelar grinned. "Already? Why, the council hasn't debated for more than several breaths. You may have achieved a new record, Regan!" Brenhold glared at the brewer. "What decisions the council has made are neither here nor there, Vindelar. Mock my cousin again and you and I shall have words on the field of honor. I think you forget your place as well as his. No matter the Judgement he is still my cousin and a member of the Royal family."

Vindelar looked at the ground, properly chastised. "Of course, My Liege. I didn't mean to offend, of course." Brenhold just glared at him as he led Regan back into the Judgement chambers.

The Judgement was passed quickly after Regan re-entered the chamber. A scroll was handed to Brenhold who then unrolled it, a momentary sad expression on his face telling Regan all he needed to know. Brenhold took a deep breath and began reading aloud.

"Regan Von Dracomarfóir, It is the opinion of this Judgement assembly that you, through no fault of your own, have lost your mental capacity to govern the Midrealm with cool objectivity and a clear head. There were many on this panel who wanted to charge you with treason as well, for speaking as you did about your ancestors and the slandering of the entire Noble element, but it was decided that, as you were not in control of your facilities, no further charges would be pressed. However, being found unfit for your inherited position as Sovereign of the realm you will be executed by being hung from your neck until you are dead five days from now, as the sun sinks below the horizon. You will be executed without benefit of hood or mask, so all may see your face and know it is not an imposter who will die in your place. Messengers will be sent out at the conclusion of these proceedings to announce your fate so all who are able will be in attendance to watch your journey into next world. May the Gods hold you close to them and allow you safe entry into their realms, for it is the belief of this panel that you are not to blame, merely an unfortunate victim of a cruel fate."

Regan listened to the announcement calmly, finally nodding as Brenhold finished reading the scroll. He met the eyes of the panel one more time and smiled. "If I go to the next realm by your Judgement I will do so with pride. When I see my Father I shall give him your regards and will plead with the Gods to see fit to be lenient with you when your day arrives for your small minds and spineless ways. I offer you proof of my sanity and you disregard my words in favor of the chance to remove someone from office who has new ideas to help everyone even though it may threaten your precious piles of gold."

He turned then and nodded to the guards. "Take me away, Gentlemen. I no longer have a desire to be kept in such a company. My hours are measured, let me spend them with the rats of the dungeon for they are are far more honorable and trustworthy company than this lot."

Chapter 22

Lucinda was tending the tables at the inn when the messenger arrived, tacking the proclamation to the wall with little ceremony and then heading on his way. The crowd in the tavern began muttering angrily among themselves when they read it. "It's not fair!" One of them exclaimed. "Yeah, We all knew Regan! He weren't crazy! This is just a put up by that rotten cousin of his!"

One of the farmers nodded in agreement angrily. "Aye! I don't care if he thought he saw a dragon or not! Regan was a good guy! It would serve them right if a dragon showed up and leveled the whole town! I'd be cheering for the lizard if it happened!"

Lucinda pushed her way through the crowd and read the announcement, gasping out loud as the words swam in front of her face. A hand was laid on her shoulder gently. "I'm sorry, Lucinda." One of the hunters spoke, looking at her sympathetically. "I know what he meant to you. I wish there was something we could do."

Lucinda paused, thinking for a moment. "Perhaps there is, Roland. The Nobles don't think we are capable of doing anything but listening to their words and doing their work for them. Perhaps it is time we showed them we are as much a voice in the realm as they are. Go, gather all you know who would see a terrible wrong avoided. Tell them to get here as soon as possible. I have someone I need to speak to, but I will be back as soon as I am able."

With that she turned and ran from the common hall, heading to her room to throw a few of her belongings in a bag.

As Lucinda hurriedly packed she felt a set of eyes upon her back. She paused and turned to face her mother. "I'm going to find the dragon, Mother. Perhaps he can still save Regan. I can't just sit by and watch him be executed for telling the truth."

Mamai nodded, looking at her daughter. "Are you certain you are willing to take these sort of risks for a man you can never be with? I overheard you talking to the hunter in the common room. Take care, child. I fear you are planning on poking a very angry bear with a very small stick."

Lucinda smiled at her mother, embracing her tightly. "Thank you for your concern, Mother, but saving Regan isn't just for me. As much as I wish we could be together, it has more to do with the fact he would be an amazing King. He has the chance to make all of our lives better and he understands us like no other King has before. He actually sees us as people, and not something on the level of the cattle in their stables!"

She set her jaw firmly, looking deeply into her mother's eyes. "If I can do something to help him I'm going to, and no one is going to stop me."

Mamai backed off, laughing, holding her hands up in submission. "Okay, Okay, Lucinda! I wasn't trying to stop you from going, I just wanted to make sure you knew what you were getting into. You're old enough to make your own decisions, my love, and it does my heart good to see you making the right ones. Go now, be safe and good luck. I'll be waiting with a nice, hot meal when you get back!"

Lucinda was soon out in the forest walking through the darkness following the same path she had followed to find Regan the first time. She was certain she could find the way again, but the moonlight had changed and fresh shadows crisscrossed the trail, soon leaving her completely lost.

She began moving faster, her eyes straining to find any sign she was headed in the right direction. Finally, completely lost and exhausted, she sat down next to a tree and began sobbing softly in frustration. She muttered angrily to herself between her sobs. "Here I am, lost in the woods like a baby who wandered from her mother and Regan is going to die in less than five days!" After crying for a bit longer she finally sat up, her back against a large tree and took a deep breath, wiping the tears from her eyes angrily.

"Well, I'm not giving up! I don't care if I have to crawl on my hands and knees, I'm finding Araseth and making him help Regan!" She stood and wrapped her hair into a quick braid, took a drink of water and stepped off into the shadows once more. Soon she stumbled across the lake, the waters glowing eerily in the reflected moonlight. She began making her way around the shore, looking carefully for the slit in the wall.

Finally, in desperation, she dared call out. "Araseth! Araseth, I need to speak to you! It's important!" Suddenly a light appeared in front of her. One of the faerie glared at her, stamping her foot silently while she flitted in the air. She made a shushing gesture and pointed across the lake.

Lucinda could just barely make out the flickering light of a campfire. It was a mere dot off on the horizon, flicking like a fallen star, but it was there. Realizing what it might mean Lucinda gasped, covering her mouth. "I'm so sorry! I didn't know there was anyone else around! Could you lead me to Araseth? Its of the utmost importance!" The little faerie looked thoughtful for a moment, looking back over at the campfire. Finally she nodded and motioned Lucinda to follow her. The girl moved as quietly as possible, following the little shimmering light to the dragon.

The great beast raised an eyebrow curiously as Lucinda entered the hidden valley.

"And what brings King Regan's true love to visit an old beast during the deep darkness of the night?" He rumbled softly from his favorite perch on top of the broken rock.

She looked up at him and began speaking, her voice cracking despite herself. "Araseth.. I.. they.. Regan is going to be executed in three days! You have to do something! They've sent out messengers and I have hunters gathering but I don't know if we'll get there in time and .. "

Araseth looked at her coolly, finally raising a single claw to silence her. "Slowly, human girl. These ears are far too old to comprehend rambling words. Now, start once more and tell me what is wrong slowly."

Lucinda took a deep breath, calmed a bit by the Dragon's words. "Regan has been tried for lunacy since he was overheard speaking to his father about you. He was judged guilty and has been sentenced to hang three days from now. I have sent hunters to summon people who will try to help, but I fear it will not be enough. A dragon showing up before his execution may, perhaps, save his life."

Araseth lowered his head and sighed sadly. "I warned him not to tell the truth of me to anyone. I knew any mention of my continued life would bring death upon both our heads. What could have possibly motivated the boy to speak so?"

Lucinda shrugged. "I know not, Lord Dragon, although I am sure he had good reason to break your trust. All I know is a man who would be a King to be remembered is about to be executed by his own people for believing in you. You must go! Prove to the people he is not a lunatic and that you are real! Show the Kingdom the glory which is Araseth!"

The dragon glared down at her from his perch in the high rocks. "I cannot, girl child!" He spat, angrily. "Do you not understand? The last time I saw a human besides Regan I was shot by onyx arrows and stabbed repeatedly until all I was able to do was lay there and watch my brood be slaughtered in front of me. Now those terrible weapons are once again removed from the armory! Even as we speak there are mercenaries in the pay of a man named Vindelar out scouring the forest for me. Luckily Marimo and the other faeries heard the men setting up camp and they spied on them for me so I know their intent. I have no choice now. I cannot help Regan. His unfortunate telling of stories better off left unspoken has undone us both. I am afraid he will have to face his Judgement. You found me as I was preparing to leave, Lucinda. I will ask the Gods to keep watch for Regan, but I have no desire to taste foul onyx once more merely to make a futile gesture."

Lucinda stared at the great beast incredulously. "You are leaving then? Abandoning the man you called friend to face the hangman's noose alone?" She set her jaw angrily. "Well, he will not be alone, Dragon. Regan will have his followers there. There are those of us who would be willing to die because it is the right thing to do. Luckily there are still some of us with a backbone. To think, as a child I was terrified of your kind. Now I grow into a woman only to find the Great Dragon is no more brave or fierce than the snake who slithers under my feet. Go then! We will win the day or lose it, it matters not, for we will go into the next realm with our heads held high knowing we did our best while you are stuck in this realm, safe in whatever hole you find to hide in, forced to live each day with your cowardice!"

Just then a loud, grinding noise was heard and rocks began tumbling from the wall of the concealed passage. A scream of pain was heard from inside while a hundred tiny lights flickered above. Araseth's head jerked upward, his every sense alert. "They've found me." He said softly. "Your cries have given them a clue as to where I am. I must depart immediately!"

A gleaming, ebony tipped arrow sang past his head as he looked down at Lucinda. "Get on my back, Child. I will carry you to your home before I depart this realm forever."

She glared up at him and shook her head stubbornly. "I would crawl before I would accept a favor from you, Coward!"

Another arrow sang past, striking a brilliant spark on the rock next to the dragon's head. "If you do not climb upon my back you will never make it back to your inn in time." He said simply, stretching his wings in preparation to fly. Lucinda looked at the men advancing through the opening, all shouting in excitement at seeing the great beast for the first time. She grabbed his neck and swung aboard his back. "Very well, I will accept your charity, Dragon." She hissed into his ear. "But do not mistake that for forgiveness for your cowardly act!"

Araseth leaped into the air, Lucinda gasping at the suddenness of the ascent. Onyx tipped arrows sang as they sliced the air around them. She felt the dragon lurch as one of them pierced his wing and he hissed in agony. Then they were away, tearing through the night. Lucinda held on desperately since the wounded wing was causing Araseth to fly erratically. Finally he wheeled and landed, roughly, in a clearing just down the road from the inn. He hissed again as he attempted to fold his wounded wing, finally leaving it dragging on the ground.

"I will leave you now, Lucinda." He said simply, looking at the girl. "I wish you the Gods' blessing in your venture. I truly hope you can save Regan. He is far to good a man to die because of a cowardly old dragon." He looked away then, not able to meet her eyes any longer. "Perhaps some day you will find it in your heart to forgive me for not going to save him, but I truly hope you will never have to feel the pain which would make you understand why I do what I do."

He leaped into the air then, a flurry of wind buffering the girl as he clawed desperately toward the sky, trying to get enough elevation to fly away. She watched him depart and sighed, sadly. She had begun to understand the agony the single tiny arrow caused him, the pain from multiple wounds must have been unbearable. Finally he disappeared into the sky and she turned, heading into the inn to meet whatever others had gathered.

As she walked into the common room she was surprised to see so many people crowded in. Farmers, hunters, cart drivers, even a couple of wandering minstrels in from Secondrealm, judging by the looks of their outfits.

She paused as she entered the room. Hopeful faces turned toward her expectantly. Finally Gruunar, one of the millers from down the road asked the question they were all waiting for. "Well? Did you find the dragon? Is it real? Is he going to help us?"

She shot her mother a dirty look then she shook her head and sighed. "No. The dragon is gone. He is real, but he has left. Vindelar sent mercenaries out to hunt him down and kill him, so he has gone forever. If we are going to save King Regan it will be up to us."

A mummer rolled across the room, people shaking their heads doubtfully. "Its only us, Lucinda! What do you think we can do to stop a whole army?" She shook her head in frustration. "I don't know, but we have to do something." Her eyes scanned the room desperately, finally landing on one of the hunters leaning on his bow. "And I think I may just have an idea."

Chapter 23

The dawn brightened on a beautiful day when Regan was due to be executed. He awoke early, washed himself, and sat by the window to gaze over the open fields, watching the sun rise slowly into the sky and the few thick, white clouds moving past the window like great sailing vessels, bound for nowhere. He sighed, realizing the sun's passage was counting down the hours until he was to die. He was allowed to stay in his own chambers for the days before his execution. He had access to parchment and ink so he wrote.

He had written night and day the first 2 days, recording every single thing he could remember from the dragon's stories. He smiled when he thought of Marimo, the first time she had landed on his knee to listen to one of Araseth's tales. He looked over at the rolls of sealed parchments and sighed.

Likely they would all be burned after his execution. They contained a story that far to many of those in power wanted forgotten. A knock came on his door, likely his breakfast. "Come." He said simply, not really wanting anyone's company, but feeling the pangs of hunger after going for four days without much to eat. The door swung open and someone walked inside the room, closing the door. His jaw dropped open in shock. "Lucinda? But.. How can this be?"

She gave her sarcastic half smile and walked over to him, taking his hands in hers. "Apparently your door guard has a particular fondness for Mother's meat pies. I bribed him with three of them to let me see you for the time it took him to eat them, so I will be quick because he seemed to be a rather piggish man."

Regan shook his head in wonder, staring at her in admiration. "Lucinda, you are most definitely the most incredible woman I have ever known. I will die happy tonight, having seen your face one last time." She smiled and shook her head, leaning close to his ear so her lips brushed it lightly. "No you won't, Regan.. Because we are going to get you out of here."

Regan frowned in confusion, looking around. "What do you mean we?" He asked softly. "I only see the love of my life standing before me." She slapped him lightly on the shoulder. "Not now, Silly King." She said mockingly. "Tonight. Before the execution. And then you and I are going to leave. There is a boat waiting for us. We're going to go away until we can prove your sanity and it is safe to come back again."

Regan stared into her eyes and smiled lovingly at her for a long moment before shaking his head negatively. "No, Lucinda." He said softly. "I will not have you risking your life for me. I am honored more than words can say by you planning to do this, but I could not bear the thought of you coming to harm because of me. I fear Brenhold was right. I am not made correctly to be a good King. Let my foolishness rest after tonight. I will go in peace knowing you are well and Araseth is safe."

Lucinda stepped back from Regan, her eyes wide. "Oh! You haven't heard yet! I completely forgot! Araseth isn't safe, Regan! A man named Vindelar has hired mercenaries to hunt him down and destroy him. They were armed with onyx weapons and he fled!"

Regan frowned deeply at the news. "So the weasel believed every word I said and has made an effort to remove the dragon before anyone else can find him." He thought for a moment, finally nodding. "Very well, My Love, let me hear your plan. I fear even if they kill me Araseth will be hunted to the end of the world and destroyed. We must not allow that to happen."

By the time the guard had finished the meat pies Lucinda had explained the plan to Regan who nodded in approval.

"Brilliant, My Dear!" He said, grinning. "Remind me if I ever regain the throne to make you my armies' main strategist!" Lucinda beamed with pride and kissed Regan gently on the lips. "Let's just hope it works, Regan. I've grown awfully fond of your face and I would hate to have to see it all purple and swollen hanging off a rope."

Regan made a face at her. "Well, thank you very much, Lucinda. I am quite madly in love with you too!"

The guard entered the room and motioned to Lucinda. "All right, Miss. Time to go. I'll be lucky if I don't get in trouble as it is!" Lucinda nodded and smiled at the guard. "Of course. I was just finishing saying my goodbyes. Thank you again for being so kind to let me see him!"

She swept out the door with a wink back at Regan. The hefty guard shook his head sorrowfully. "Regan, I have to say, I sure am sorry about all this. I think you would have made a great King and if you would have had a whit of sense you would have changed the laws so you could have married that girl!"

Regan nodded to the guard, clapping him on the shoulder. "You're one of the good ones, Bernand. I'll put in a good word for you with the Gods when I enter their realm."

He guided the guard to the door and closed it behind him. He moved over and sat on the edge of his bed once again, looking out at the brilliant sunshine. Suddenly the large ball in the sky didn't look as much like a huge, flaming reaper, coming to take him away.

Chapter 24

An hour before sunset they came for him. Three guards in full military dress knocked on his door and then swung it open.

"Regan, it is time. Are you ready to face the Gods?" Regan stood slowly and nodded. "I am, Gentlemen. I am at peace with my fate. You may lead me to the gallows, I will not try to resist."

They led him down then, through the halls of the castle and through the entrance. He was stunned by the throngs of people in the courtyards. Children sat on father's shoulders, straining to see him, merchants sold fruit and candied nuts, the maidens of the court waved their silken scarves at him as he passed them.

He leaned to one of the guards and whispered into his ear. "Am I to be hanged or honored tonight?" The guard chuckled as they walked. "They all want to come and send you off proper, Highness. Most people feel like you don't deserve what you're getting so they want the Gods to hear them cheering for you so they open the gates wide and let you in."

Regan nodded, walking up the steps to the platform, a single black silken rope hanging in a noose from the gallows frame. He stepped up to it and when the executioner moved to place it around his neck, he waved him away, placing the soft noose around his neck himself while looking out at the crowd. He heard the exclamations of the people as he did so.

Brenhold stepped onto the stage, dressed in his finest robes. He looked sympathetically at Regan for a moment. "I am sorry, Cousin. I truly never wanted this to happen." Regan shrugged, smiling. "Just so you know, Bren, I always thought you would make a better King than I myself. You always had the right.. stuffiness for it." Brenhold shook his head in amazement. "The end of your life and you still joke. Gods keep you safe, Regan. Tell our ancestors I greet them and I will see them when it is my time."

He placed his hand on his cousin's shoulder for a moment before turning to the crowd. He cleared his throat and addressed them. "On this gallows before you stands Regan Von Dracomarfóir, The Rightful King of the Midrealm. He is being executed tonight through no fault of his own, merely because he does not have the capacity for leadership any longer. Although fate has been cruel and robbed him of his sanity as per the Judgement, let no man, woman or child in attendance or in the realm, speak ill of him. The highest law of the land states when a Sovereign no longer has the capacity to lead he will be executed in the most humane way possible so no man can use his unstable state in an attempt to gain control of the Throne.

These laws have been placed since the beginning of our rule and thus they remain today. Let any who care to walk before these gallows and look into his face, so they can make no claim hereafter this was not the man who was Judged."

With that Brenhold stepped to the side to allow the forming line a clear view of Regan's face. He stood stoically, looking down at them as they passed before him. The sun sank lower on the horizon as the throngs moved past. Regan could tell which ones had a part in the moment because, unlike the expressions of sympathy or sorrow on most people's faces, they looked away and refused to meet the eyes of the man they had condemned to death.

Finally the line ended, the sun sinking slowly under the horizon. Regan shifted nervously, looking for any sign the rescue was on its way in the deepening shadows. A strong breeze came up, the evening winds which blew across the realm every night just at sunset. Brenhold took a deep breath and looked at Regan one more time. "Goodbye cousin." He said softly, turning to the executioner and nodding. The executioner reached for the lever and wrapped his hand around it, beginning to pull it to release the trap door and drop Regan to his death when suddenly a cry rang put from the crowd.

"By the GODS! Look! Up there! It's a DRAGON!" The crowd tuned as one to look into the sky. There, wings flapping in the breeze as it hovered, was a great black mass.

"That's not a dragon!" Another voice sang out, "Where are the flames?" Just then the shadowy form opened its mouth and a large gout of flame poured from it's gaping jaws. The crowd let out another loud gasp, which covered the sound of the arrow striking the release mechanism, jamming it.

Regan heard a pair of boots on the platform behind him, a razor sharp blade slicing cleanly through the silken rope. "Let's get out of here, Love." Lucinda whispered, half dragging Regan from the platform. "Wait!" Another voice cried out from the crowd.

"Look! Its head is on fire! That is no dragon! Its only bits of cloth and a firepot made up to look like one!" Regan glanced up at the floating form as it was quickly enveloped in flames. It fell to the ground in a shower of sparks, all eyes turning to the gallows. Lucinda and Regan were surrounded by the guards quickly, a wall of drawn swords preventing their escape.

The archer, one of the hunters Regan knew, was led from the tower where he had waited until just the right moment to fire the arrow which had blocked the lever. Brenhold approached Regan and shook his head sadly. "It was a good attempt, Cousin. It nearly worked. You might have escaped if the kite hadn't caught fire. Perhaps a mere accident, or perhaps the Gods calling you home, where you belong. I am only sorry you dragged others into your lunatic fantasies. Now you are going to have to explain at the gates why there are others in your presence. You know the rules, Cousin. All who tried to assist you will now share your fate."

Regan looked over at Lucinda, his eyes wide with fear. "No.. Cousin.. Sire! I beg you! I will die. I will take my own life if need be, but spare the ones who tried to help me. It was not their fault. I ordered them to rescue me while I was still King. They were merely following my commands!"

Lucinda looked at Regan angrily and slapped him hard, across the face. She turned to Brenhold defiantly. "Regan lies to protect me, Your Majesty. It was by my own will I tried to save him and by my own will I choose to die beside him. All of us here tonight knew what risks we took and all of us would rather die than continue to live in this foul, corrupt society. Dragons are real, King Brenhold, and one day they will return to this realm to seek vengeance for all of the wrongs which have been done to them, and to us. My only regret is I will not still be alive to watch this kingdom burn! I hope you are still alive to watch the dragon fire consume the castle around you and as it falls to pieces you begin to understand how wrong you were about your cousin!"

Brenhold shook his head sadly looking at the girl for a moment before turning away. "Guards, two more ropes on the gallows. And replace the one for Regan as well. No need for silk this time, he has proven himself beneath those courtesies."

Soon the three of them stood, shoulder to shoulder, nooses around their necks, looking out at the crowd.

Brenhold faced them sadly. Then shook his head one final time and turned his back on them. He addressed the crowd once more. "For crimes against this court and attempting to disrupt an official execution Regan Von Dracomarfóir and his cohorts must die. Are there any here who would speak against this sentencing and thus, decide to join with them?"

The crowd was completely silent, all watching. The muffled sobs of Mamai could be heard at the back of the court as she hung onto her husband for comfort, her face buried in his chest.

"Then, as it is my duty as Sovereign of the Midrealm I sentence you all to death. May the God's be merciful to your spirits!"

He turned and started to motion to the executioner to pull the handle and he froze, staring off into the sky. High above the castle, coming closer every minute was not one, but ten huge dark forms. As they approached streams of fire blasted from their mouths, crimson streaks of brilliant light blazing through the night sky.

They circled above the castle in perfect formation, the full moon gleaming brightly off their scales. Brenhold stood and stared for a moment, completely frozen in shock. "By the Gods.." he muttered finally. "Dragons..."

As everyone stood transfixed one man slipped away from the crowd. Vindelar moved quickly through the tunnels on his way out of the castle. He hurriedly tucked Regan's tightly rolled scroll into a pouch as he ran, jumping on a horse and heading off toward the mountains.

One of the massive black forms finally separated from the rest, dropping to the castle wall and perching, his wounded wing resting a bit awkwardly at his side. He tilted his head upward and shot a great gout of fire into the sky before announcing in a voice so loud it rattled the walls,

"I am Araseth, Lord of all Dragonkind. I come to give this castle and those who lead its people fair warning. If any harm comes to the one known as Regan we will melt this castle and all who dwell within it to ash. We have no wish to do so, but neither will we allow another to suffer for our existence."

The huge dragon craned his neck around, looking down at Brenhold. "This is the point in which you order your men to free him, King." He said quietly.

Brenhold merely nodded, his mouth open in shock, and then looked over at the guards. "Free the prisoners." He said softly. The ropes came off their necks and everyone looked around awkwardly for a moment. Suddenly Regan ripped one of the guard's daggers from his belt and flung it toward Brenhold. The razor sharp blade wheeled past his cousin's neck and the King Temporum dove out of the way. A sharp exclamation of pain followed and Regan followed the dagger's flight off the platform to grab one of the mercenary hunters who had been drawing back an onyx tipped arrow to let fly at Araseth.

He dragged the warrior back onto the platform and shook him soundly. The man grasped his wounded arm in pain. Regan cupped him under the chin and turned his face upward, forcing him to look into the former King's eyes.

"Who paid you and armed you with these weapons, Soldier?" He demanded, giving the wounded man another shake for good measure. "Speak, before I use one of these ropes for the purpose in which it was intended!"

The man blanched slightly, glancing over at the still swinging nooses. "It was Vindelar, Sire. He was the one what paid us to hunt down and kill a dragon. It was him that give us those weapons, too."

Regan dropped the man and turned angrily to the crowd. "There. You all heard. The man who accused me of lunacy was so convinced by my story he hired mercenaries to hunt and kill the dragon he said only existed in my mind! Now, FIND him and bring him to me! I want Vindelar in front of me NOW!"

Soon all guards were searching the castle hastily, looking for a sign of the small brewer. Regan turned to Brenhold and

The Dragon King

smiled. "Cousin, It gives me great pleasure to present Araseth, Lord of all Dragonkind. " He turned and looked up at Araseth gratefully. "Araseth, My cousin, King Brenhold."

Araseth nodded his head regally, acknowledging Brenhold gracefully. Regan grinned and reached up, taking the crown from Brenhold's head. "If I may borrow this for a moment, Cousin. After all, my claims have apparently been

proven, therefore the Judgement is void, which, unless I am mistaken, makes me King again."

Brenhold nodded and smiled. "Yes, I believe it does, KING Regan." He bowed deeply and grinned. "A pleasure to serve you, Milord!"

Regan set the crown upon his head and turned, facing the milling crowd in the courtyard. He cleared his throat for attention, although no one seemed to notice. Finally he sighed, gesturing to the Royal trumpeters who brought their instruments up and blew a loud tone to get everyone's attention. Everyone stopped and stared at the gallows the King was standing on.

Regan smiled and raised his arms. "Nobles and commoners, Lords, Ladies and all other good people of the Kingdom. I will ask you now to hear my words, for they will become the new law of this land." He paused, looking around to make sure he had everyone's attention. "My first decree, as reinstated King Temporum, is that no man, woman or child living in this land shall ever cause harm to one of our friends, the Dragons, now or in the future. As of now I am asking them to join us and become knights of this realm with all of the rights and privileges incurred. If ANYONE is found causing undue harm to one of the new citizens they will incur the full wrath of this court and will be Judged to the maximum penalty of our laws. In addition the Faerie folk will fall under this protection as well. They are to be granted all rights and privileges of full citizens and will no longer be required to hide in the woodlands like animals, but will be welcomed as equals in our settlements."

As he spoke those words tiny lights began to blink on all around the castle. The people of the realm gasped softly in shock as the tiny faeries appeared among them, their faint lights glowing brighter. One of them flew up to Regan and curtsied deeply, smiling. Regan grinned back.

"Hello, Marimo. I'm glad you could make it tonight!"

He turned back to the crowd once again. "My SECOND decree of this night.. For heroism above and beyond the call of King and country, for putting her life on the line for what she believed in, I name Lucinda of the Vale Baroness and grant her the lands on which the Day's ride Inn reside as well as the surrounding forest. AND since this newly appointed Baroness is now Royalty under the King's command, it is completely allowable by law that I ask her if she would consider binding our spirits together in marriage."

He looked over at Lucinda and grinned. She stood shocked for a moment and then ran over to him, wrapping her arms around him tightly. The crowd cheered wildly as he kissed her. Finally they broke the kiss and he turned once again to the crowd, this time holding Lucinda close to him.

"For my third and final decree of the night- I now take the power of King and halve it. I name Brenhold Sovereign of Daily Affairs. From this day forward we will share the responsibility of Leadership to the people of this land. We will discuss and argue and find a new way for things to be where all will truly have the chance to live in equality with each other."

He looked over at Brenhold and smiled. "That is, if you're up to the challenge, Cousin." Brenhold chuckled and nodded, shrugging. "Why not? We've been arguing all of our lives, we may as well continue a while longer."

Regan looked up at Araseth and grinned widely. "Now, Sir Knight, Would you and the rest of your party care to join us in a feast in celebration of my engagement?" Araseth chuckled, the old familiar sound of two rocks scraping together. "We would be honored, My King."

He threw back his head and cried out, the dragons landing gently one by one in the courtyard. Regan raised an eyebrow when he saw a smaller dragon land protectively next to Araseth. He could have sworn he saw the large dragon blush a bit as he introduced her.

"King Regan, this is Belasith. She is the one who helped bind my wing when I landed in Secondrealm. Belasith, This is King Regan, the one I told you of who has the spirit to change the world."

Regan smiled and bowed deeply. "I am truly happy to meet you, Belasith, and I owe you a debt of thanks. I fear if it were not for your timely arrival I would be swinging by my neck at the moment."

Regan winced. "Oh, Drat! I meant to mention we would be rebuilding Mhirachor once again!" Araseth chuckled. "There is no need, Sire. We flew over Mhirachor on the way here. It is as splendid and perfect as the day it was finished."

Regan smiled and nodded. Lucinda whistled softly. "So.. the Prophecy has come true! The castle of the Dragon rises once more!" She paused, thinking. "But.. that means.." Regan shook his head gently, kissing her lightly on the lips. "A worry for another day, My love. Come, let us go celebrate wonderful friends with better timing and glorious days ahead!"

Chapter 25

Vindelar rode through the forest wildly, his horse frothing with sweat from his mad dash from the castle. Finally he stopped and built a small fire for the night. As he sat with his back to a tree he took out the scroll Regan had carefully written, looking it over until he saw a small drawing of a map showing a certain volcanic slide.

He turned the map a bit, orienting himself and then grinned. "Some of us are meant to have, Regan, and some of us are not." He muttered under his breath, glancing up at the pick and shovel strapped to the horse. "Let us see how your New Realm fares when the dark horde rises once more."

Epilogue

When the old man finally stopped speaking he looked down at his grandson and smiled. "And now you know the story, Eban. Do you agree with me that it was a very important story that only a boy on the verge of becoming a man should hear?"

Eban nodded, grinning widely, his head still spinning a bit from listening to the story. "I think that was the best story I've ever heard, Grandpa!" He said, enthusiastically. "Are there more tales about Araseth and Regan? I want to hear all of them!"

His grandfather nodded and chuckled. "Oh yes, there are many more of them, Eban. They had a wonderful long friendship and shared many adventures together. Perhaps I will tell you more another day, if you'd like."

Eban nodded, excited, and picked up his cup of long cold cocoa and took a sip of it. He tilted his head, thinking for a moment as he shifted a bit on the old bearskin rug. "Grandpa? How do you know these stories? You tell stories like no one I've ever heard before. It is like you were there, like you were watching when Araseth came swooping down to save Regan. NO one tells stories the way you do!"

Grandpa chuckled softly, gazing into the crackling fire for a moment, lost in his thoughts. Finally, his lips twisted into an odd smile and he looked back at his grandson, his eyes shining brightly. "Well, Eban, Perhaps I'll tell you someday. It is quite a fascinating story, and you deserve to hear it. But that's a story for another time."

END

The Dragon King

ACKNOWLEDGMENTS

First: To both of our families, for putting up with posing for pictures, allowing us to take time away from them while we worked, and all other inconveniences. Second: To all of our cheerleaders: Berill, Catherine, and all the rest who kept us going when we may have otherwise given up. Third, I would like to thank, as the author, Laurie Ragan who had the vision to make the world real and the confidence in me to allow me to attempt to describe her world.

ABOUT THE AUTHOR

Dan Williams had always dreamed of being a writer. Living in Alaska and working a regular job he put those dreams to the side until his wife, Glenda, was involved in a fatal accident and he was forced to re-evaluate his life. Attending Full Sail University reignited his passion for the written word and when Laurie approached him with an idea for a book based on some of her paintings it was too much to resist. Thus, the Dragon King was born.

ABOUT THE ILLUSTRATOR

Laurie Ragan answered the artistic call early in life, taking up her box of crayons and drawing at the age of three. In 1974, after her first son was born Laurie began teaching herself to paint. Over the years she has developed her own unique style of art, designing and painting many murals as well as countless original works all of which have culminated in the creation of the world of The Dragon King, a rich fantasy world populated by many close family members.

21066378R00083

Made in the USA
San Bernardino, CA
04 May 2015